TRAPPING THE BUTTERFLY

DEBRA PARMLEY

Text Copyright © 2015 by Debra Parmley
Cover Art Copyright by Belo Dia Publishing Inc. © 2017 Cover Artist: Sheri L. McGathy

Published by Belo Dia Publishing Inc.
P.O. Box Ellendale, TN 38135

Published in the United States of America
Third Edition

 Created with Vellum

This book is dedicated to all the young girls who long to emerge from their cocoons as independent women.

May your wings be strong and may you safely reach your happy ever after.

Start with a resort location, throw in a famous gangster with a detective hot on his trail, add a Jazz age setting, and you've got the makings for a fun read. Trapping the Butterfly has that and more, taking the reader on a Roaring Twenties tour through Hot Springs, Arkansas where the rich and famous traveled to "take the cure." ...The author ... describes what the spa treatments were like ... shows how life was changing in America, especially for young women. Overall, I enjoyed my visit to Hot Springs with this charming Jazz age story.

— -LONG AND SHORT REVIEWS

CHAPTER ONE

AUGUST 1926

*B*ethany Robinson did not need yet another lecture on being appreciative.

"Thank you, Aunt Margaret." She accepted the gold trimmed, white china plate her aunt handed her while clearing her throat to disguise the grumbling of her stomach. Placing the plate in front of her on the table, she waited and tried not to look at the food placed upon it.

At the head of the table, Uncle James cut a large bite of chicken and popped it into his mouth without waiting for anyone. Aunt Margaret said nothing, but straightened her fork with that look upon her face, her lips puckering like a prune. She straightened the fork again, showing her blue veins and the bones beneath her thin, pale skin.

Aunt Margaret was in a mood, and she obviously wasn't going to say Grace.

So it would be one of *those* kinds of meals. If only Bethany could have eaten in the kitchen, with cook as she'd been allowed to when she was younger.

She glanced down at her chicken, wondering if it was safe to eat a bite or if that would draw her aunt's attention and sour mood. *Perhaps it would be best to wait.* The tension in the room gathered closer, and the more she could distance herself from that, the better.

Her stomach rumbled again.

"Margaret," Uncle James said. "Please eat something."

Her aunt, a small, bird-like woman, who barely ate enough to keep a bird alive, said, "I couldn't eat a bite."

Such a predictable old refrain.

"Not a thing." Aunt Margaret sighed. "You go on, dear. Take it." She held out her plate to him, looking away from it as if the food offended her. "I simply can't."

Bethany would have loved for her aunt to have offered *her* the savory chicken she'd passed over to Uncle James, but she said nothing and instead cut her own portion into small pieces and ate one slow bite so as not to draw attention to herself.

Having an entire breast of chicken all for herself just once would be nice. Her aunt always cut the chicken breasts in half.

One might fill her up. If anything could.

Bethany suspected Aunt Margaret counted how many bites Bethany took. Though counting bites was something Bethany did, too, it was different when she did it.

Four more bites, see? Out of five. If she chewed them slowly enough, she might feel full faster. Strange how that sometimes worked. That, and drinking lots of water.

Though not today. Not the way Aunt Margaret stared at her with that look, her brown eyes darkening like storm clouds gathering.

Thump.

"Enough!" Uncle James thumped his fist on the table again, his fork still in his hand.

Both women turned to him in surprise.

"Enough. I am taking you to Hot Springs National Park for the baths, and you will not argue with me."

Bethany raised one eyebrow. He wasn't talking to her. She never argued with Uncle James. *What was he talking about? What did he mean by enough?*

"One likes to be asked." Aunt Margaret sniffed and her facial expression turned haughty. "There is no need to speak to a lady in that tone, Mr. Robinson."

"Mrs. Robinson, I am asking you to travel with me to the medicinal springs to partake of the baths and healing properties of the waters." His tone brooked no argument and said just as clearly that he was not asking, but telling.

"I will think about it."

Uncle James, knowing as well as Bethany did, that the phrase Aunt Margaret had just used meant *no,* then changed both his tone and his approach. "I am asking out of concern for you, dear. Your health is no better and seems to be getting worse."

"I have done everything the doctor asked."

"Yes, and now we are going to try a new doctor. One who has had success with women in your condition."

What exactly was that condition? They always referred to it as *one of Aunt Margaret's spells.* Maybe this new doctor would finally have a name for it.

"The trip will do you good, and I have a meeting with Mr. Rivalde after we arrive."

"About the merger we've been discussing?" She glanced over at Bethany then back again.

"Yes. He is amiable."

"Well, then." Aunt Margaret sniffed. "We shall all go to Hot Springs and take the baths." She shot a pointed glance at Bethany.

Bethany placed her hands in her lap and folded her fingers together. "When are we going?"

"Next week," Uncle James said. "We'll take a two week holiday." He nodded at his wife again. "That should be long enough."

Aunt Margaret nodded in agreement.

Would two weeks be long enough to cure her aunt? *That didn't seem like very long. Oh, but if we're gone that long...*

"That means we'll be away on my birthday," Bethany blurted out, and then stopped herself from saying more.

This would be her eighteenth birthday. She'd moved from counting down the months to counting the weeks left. Soon she would be of age and no longer under Aunt Margaret's thumb.

"We'll celebrate your birthday in Hot Springs. That will make it a very memorable trip." Aunt Margaret smiled a secretive smile.

That smile would have made Bethany nervous had they *not* been discussing her birthday.

Just a week left to plan before they left for Hot Springs, Arkansas.

Bethany would have to change her original idea, but she would still go through with it. Nothing short of illness or death would stop her from carrying out her plan.

Being in Hot Springs might even make it easier.

BETHANY HAD NEVER BEEN inside the train station before. She peered out beneath her wide brimmed hat as she looked about taking in the sights and sounds around her.

Her aunt resembled a crow in a tailored black worsted jersey suit, gray hat, and black shoes as she darted her gaze about the station, looking for an open space on one of the wooden benches.

Not for the first time, Bethany noticed how old fashioned her aunt appeared in the skirt that came nearly to her ankles. The suit was at least five years old, and her aunt wouldn't replace it until it wore out. Despite the fact Mr. Robinson owned his own company and moved among the wealthier members of society, his frugal wife stretched every penny and clung to the older fashions.

Most of the women bustling about the station wore newer fashions and shorter skirts. Bethany glanced down at her own navy blue georgette crepe frock which fell well below the knee, the long, lacy collar the only pretty thing she liked about it. At least with her wide brimmed hat, she could duck her head and hide when she wanted to.

Oh, what she wouldn't give to wear one of those shorter dropped waist dresses with a cloche hat and bobbed hair. To look like other girls her age and to go dancing with boys. She could not wait for the day when she could pick out her own clothes and go when and where she wanted. Soon she would be eighteen and would be able to use her inheritance. She hoped. Uncle James had always been vague about the terms of the will and monies her parents had left behind for her.

"Come along," Aunt Margaret said, interrupting her thoughts. "We will sit and wait for your uncle."

"Yes, ma'am."

Bethany followed her aunt, who had noticed an open spot on one of the benches and strode toward it determined to claim it for her own. People moved away from her when she was in that mood and held that look upon her face. Her aunt, tiny as she was, could be a formidable woman. Soon she and Bethany sat together on a high backed wooden bench.

People bustled around the train station, many carrying newspapers and reading the headlines as they walked.

Everyone else appeared to be reading the paper. *Something must have happened.*

A long line of passengers stretched around the newspaper stand, and more joined the line as soon as it started to shorten.

Whatever had happened must have been awful. Women cried, and men shook their heads and looked mournful.

Bethany strained to see a newspaper held by a man nearby.

The headline read, *Rudolph Valentino Dead, August 23, 1926. Sudden Death at the Age of Thirty-One.*

Oh, no. He couldn't be dead. He'd just had an operation a week ago. His latest movie had just come out, and he'd gone to New York to promote it. He was too young to be dead. So young and handsome. How could Rudolph Valentino be dead?

A tear formed in the corner of Bethany's eye. Uncle James sat down next to her, and she asked, "Uncle James, are you going to buy a newspaper?"

"What for?" He frowned. Uncle James read the business news and kept up daily with Wall Street, but rarely followed stories unless they were about money or politics.

"To read about what happened to Rudolph Valentino."

"You want to read about the death of some movie star?" Uncle James directed his frown at her.

"Well, yes. Everyone is mourning him. Can't you see?"

"He must have been a drinker," Aunt Margaret said. "That's what happens to wild young men who drink."

"Hollywood types," Uncle James said with disdain. "They all drink."

"The women, too. It's disgraceful." Aunt Margaret nodded.

Both she and Uncle James were in favor of prohibition and looked down on lawbreakers. Aunt Margaret always pointed out how all the good churches now served grape juice in place of communion wine.

"No, there's nothing in that paper I wish to read."

Uncle James pulled out his pocket watch to look at it, signaling the discussion was closed.

"Young women today..." Aunt Margaret paused and let the word trail away. "I simply don't understand them."

The dark haired flapper who had drawn Aunt Margaret's attention walked by, cigarette holder in hand, as if on cue to emphasize Aunt Margaret's point.

"Drinking, smoking, running wild." Aunt Margaret tsked, then sniffed and turned her head away from the flapper, dismissing the thin, vivacious girl who was now talking with friends.

Ignoring Aunt Margaret, Bethany fingered her clutch purse. She'd saved for months to collect the money inside it. Though she yearned for a newspaper, she knew that if she bought one, it meant dipping into her fund.

Best not to dip into it for anything, or her plan might fail.

"I blame the parents," Aunt Margaret said. "You are a fortunate young lady. Why if we hadn't taken you in? Who knows what might have happened to you?"

"Yes, ma'am. Thank you." The words slipped out automatically, the pattern long established from ten years of similar conversations.

Bethany looked about the room, taking in that her aunt and uncle seemed to be the only people in the train station uninterested in the death of Rudolph Valentino.

Was the whole world mourning his death? Everyone, except perhaps Aunt Margaret and Uncle James.

At least here, Bethany didn't feel so all alone, as if no one understood her or her feelings. As if no one felt the way she did, and that she had something wrong with her.

Here, she felt more normal.

Maybe someone would leave a newspaper when they were done, and she could pick it up and read their copy.

Unfortunately, the train arrived before that happened, and the conductor called all aboard.

A movie poster beside the door where they went out to board the train advertised Valentino's final movie. It read, *Rudolph Valentino stars with Vilma Banky in The Son of the Sheikh, from the novel by E.M. Hull.*

How romantic. What an adventure a trip to a foreign land would be. To have a Sheik fall in love with you and sweep you away.

Bethany sighed.

Oh, how she wanted to see the movie. Everyone had been talking about it since it had premiered in California in July. Then the promotional tour had taken the stars across the country, and Rudolph Valentino had ended up in New York having his operation. Now, he was dead.

Bethany might never have a chance to see one of his movies.

She sat on the train in their private compartment in the window seat looking out at the world and wondering when, where, and how she would ever find her place in it. Someplace where she fit in, and where at least one person understood her.

She wanted to see *The Son of the Sheikh* so badly. The movie was supposed to open next week at home. Any day now, and everyone would see it but her.

Once again, she would miss out. She missed out on everything.

She stared out the window at the scenery. The whole world was passing her by, and right now she was powerless to do anything about it.

THEY RODE the Rock Island Railroad into Hot Springs, Arkansas, and then took a taxi to the Arlington Hotel. With two towers on top and an American flag flying in the middle, the hotel sat at the end of famous Bathhouse Row and soared impressively over all the other buildings. Bethany counted at least nine floors with windows, not counting the towers.

Their taxi let them off out front, and the taxi driver unloaded their bags for the bellman to take in. Uncle James walked up to the reception desk to check them in while Bethany waited with Aunt Margaret.

"It's beautiful," Bethany said. Inside the Lobby, two murals adorned the walls: one behind the bar on the right side of the room, and the other behind the bandstand on the left side.

Her aunt glanced about, sniffed, and said, "I hope our rooms are suitable. One never knows with a hotel."

Bethany had no frame of reference with which to compare this hotel, since she'd never been inside one before, so she remained silent and enjoyed all the new sights and sounds.

Once they finished checking in, they followed the bellman to the elevator and then accompanied him up to their rooms on the fifth floor, where he unlocked both doors. They stepped inside, and he placed their bags in their respective rooms.

Bethany hurried to the window in her room and looked out. She had an excellent view of Bathhouse Row and was high enough up to see quite far. The room was small but lovely, and she had it all to herself. Though her aunt and uncle would be right next-door, she was happy to have the privacy. She'd be able to lock the door so no one could walk in on her, not even her aunt.

"You have an hour to unpack and freshen up,

and then we'll go down to the Venetian Dining Room for dinner," Uncle James said. "Be ready."

"Yes, sir." Bethany waited until he left before spinning in a circle with her arms out and laughing. She was here inside this elegant room in Hot Springs, where her life would change forever. She could hardly wait.

The Fordyce Bathhouse, the grandest one in town, stood in the center of Bathhouse Row, on the government reservation adjoining the *Grand Entrance.* Of course this was where Uncle James had booked treatments for his wife. Only the best would do for Aunt Margaret.

Uncle James determined they would all walk to the bathhouse before their appointment with the director. Since he'd scheduled a morning appointment, the August heat had not yet reached its peak. So the walk was pleasant enough.

Bethany enjoyed taking in the colorful flowers and the tweeting of birds in the trees while walking behind her aunt and uncle as they discussed what to tell the doctor about her aunt's condition. Tired of hearing about Aunt Margaret's illness and fascinated with the many other things that caught her attention, she tuned them out.

As they passed several other bathhouses, patrons headed inside them *to take the cure.* That seemed to be the phrase on everyone's lips. If only these treatments would cure her aunt, then life would become less difficult for all of them.

They reached the front of the building, where stairs and a concrete ramp for patrons in wheelchairs led to a covered porch lined with chairs. Several patrons made their way indoors as Aunt Margaret came to a complete stop on the sidewalk.

"Dear me," she said. "I just don't know about this. I'm feeling dizzy."

"All the more reason to get you inside quickly." Uncle James grasped her by the arm. "Perhaps the walk was too much exertion for you."

Bethany wanted to roll her eyes. Their leisurely stroll from the Arlington in the morning air could hardly have been called strenuous. As usual, her aunt's symptoms worsened right before she went in to see the doctor.

Uncle James had never given any indication that he had noticed this phenomenon. He simply carried on as he was now, making sure his wife got in to see the doctor.

Bethany followed them into the lobby on the first floor and looked about. Walls of veined Italian marble rose from the floor covered with beautiful tiles, and staircases of pink marble led up to the second floor and down to the basement. A cherub fountain sat at each end of the lobby, and the stained glass over the transom windows depicted lotus blossoms. The bronze casted words beneath them read, *May health and happiness accompany you all the days of your life.*

Uncle James removed his hat before giving their names to the red headed woman at the front desk.

"Yes," she said. "Doctor Frederick is expecting you. I'll let him know you're here."

"Thank you." Uncle James nodded, and the woman stepped away from the desk. As the three of them waited in silence, the strains of piano music drifted down the stairs.

The woman returned, accompanied by Doctor Frederick.

"Mr. and Mrs. Robinson." The doctor held out his hand. "I'm Dr. Frederick. Pleased to meet you."

"Likewise," Uncle James said as the two of them shook hands.

"Please step into my office," the doctor said once they were done. "We'll discuss your wife's treatments."

The three of them followed him into the room.

"Please take a seat." He gestured to the chairs across from his desk and then walked behind it to sit.

Once they settled into their seats, he pulled out a piece of paper and laid it on his desk.

"First, I'll tell you about our facility and regimens, and then we'll discuss Mrs. Robinson's treatments."

"I've read all the pamphlets," Aunt Margaret said. "I'm anxious to hear more."

"Very good," Uncle James said.

"The bathing regimen is this: Twenty minutes in the whirlpool tub bath, with thermal water for drinking, followed by ten minutes in the sitz bath. We don't recommend the vapor cabinet for first time bathers, but you may use it during later treatments. Your attendant will draw fresh water for each bath and scrub your body with a loofah bath mitt. In between treatments, she'll wrap you in a sheet.

"In the pack room, the attendant will wrap you in steaming towels before you rest on your cot. A needle shower comes next, to cool your body after the hot packs. Then you must rest for at least thirty minutes in the cooling room until your body temperature returns to normal. If you're having a massage, you'll go to the massage room instead.

"We are very proud of our hydrotherapeutic room. It is equipped with the latest medical equipment such as sun-ray cabinets for dry heat, frigid cabinets, devices for sprays, douches, Sitz baths, electric baths, and so forth.

"For Mrs. Robinson, I recommend thirty minutes

in the sun-ray cabinet, followed by time in the frigid cabinet. We will also start her electric bath treatments within a day or two, once I see how she's progressing."

"Whatever you believe is best," Uncle James said. "I just want her to get well."

"We also have a Chiropody room and an Electro and Mechando therapy room on the second floor. Our gymnasium is on the third floor; it's open to both men and women. Don't be surprised if you run into a prizefighter or baseball player. We have all the latest equipment and treatments, and many athletes come here to train."

"Our assembly room, the ladies' parlor, and the music room are also on the third floor on the south side of the building. The gentleman's billiard room and parlor are on the north. When you finish with your treatments, you may wish to enjoy the social activities there."

He walked them out of his office and back to the front desk.

"When you arrive for each treatment, you will register here and the desk clerk will place your valuables inside one of our lock boxes." He gestured toward the brass boxes behind the desk. "She'll give you a numbered key to keep with you until you return for your things."

Uncle James nodded.

"At this point, ladies and gentlemen must part,"

the doctor continued. "Ladies enter at the south side of the building, while men enter on the north side. I cannot take you any further today, as I have another appointment this morning, so your attendants will take over once you enter the bathhouse."

"Mr. Robinson, once you enter, you should wrap your sheet around your body like a toga and sit on one of the marble benches by the fountain. You may sip mineral water while you wait."

He set a standing appointment at one o'clock every day for her aunt, prescribed a series of treatments, and assigned her an attendant.

Bethany hoped the doctor didn't expect her to accompany her aunt each day. She would have nothing to do but sit and read in the music room unless they allowed her to take a treatment, too, and she had nothing wrong with her. Other than, of course, her aunt and uncle refusing to allow her to run around with other girls her age, or heaven forbid, boys. She didn't need any treatments, but her aunt sure did.

Unfortunately, the doctor convinced her uncle that the baths would benefit everyone, including Bethany, and recommended that she have a treatment today, along with her aunt. Then tomorrow, Aunt Margaret would continue the treatments by herself. Uncle James would have a treatment today as well.

They signed in at the desk, locked away their

valuables and then Bethany and her aunt entered the south side of the building where a female attendant greeted them.

Bethany had never *taken the baths,* as everyone called it, so she wasn't sure what to expect. Doctor Frederick had explained everything to Uncle James and Aunt Martha, but Bethany had been too busy thinking of how to make her plan work to take in the details.

"I am Helga," her attendant said. "You are Bethany, ya?"

"Yes, I am."

"Follow me please."

After disrobing down to her corset, Bethany allowed Helga to unlace her and then continued undressing. She placed her clothing in the storage area and followed Helga to a private room with a bathtub. As she stepped into the deep white tub, the heat of the water overwhelmed her. Helga handed her a cup of water to drink, but that water was also hot. Still, she followed directions and drank all of it. When Helga came in and scrubbed Bethany's back with a loofah, she wasn't sure what to think... but it felt good.

"You have the pink cheeks, ya?" Without waiting for an answer, Helga put down the loofah and held out her hand. "Time to be out."

"Yes." Bethany took Helga's hand and stood. Dizziness swept over her. "Oh, goodness."

"Step down now. I wrap the towel. Then you start cooling down."

Holding tight to Helga's hand, Bethany stepped on the small stool and then onto the floor. Helga wrapped a sheet around her and led her to a lounge chair in the next room.

Bethany lay back on the lounge, and Helga wrapped hot towels around her body. Then she placed a cold, wet cloth on Bethany's forehead and handed her more water to drink.

"You drink this, ya? This will help to cool you down."

This time, the water was cooler. Once Bethany finished drinking it, Helga unwrapped her, led her into another small room, and gave her a massage.

Every little bit of tension left Bethany's body. She had never felt so good.

Tonight they were having dinner at the Arlington with a businessman Uncle James knew, a Mr. Rivalde. Yet even the idea of a long, boring evening listening to the two men talk business didn't bother Bethany now. She felt like floating, she was so relaxed.

Afterward, she dressed and waited for her aunt in the music room. She sat listening to a woman play the piano and taking in the sunshine pouring through the stained glass windows overhead that bathed the whole area in a golden glow.

"YOU'LL WANT to wear your best dress tonight, dear." Aunt Margaret pinched Bethany's cheek. "The pink one should bring out the color in your cheeks."

Weren't her cheeks already pink enough? She was still flushed from taking her bath.

"I was going to wear that one on my birthday."

"Your birthday isn't until Sunday." Aunt Margaret walked over to where Bethany had laid three of her best dresses across the bed. "Perhaps we can do a little shopping and purchase a new dress for that occasion."

"That would be nice." A new dress was bound to have more modern styling. At least a drop waist. Besides, Bethany hadn't had a new dress in well over a year. The seamstress who made their dresses always listened to Aunt Margaret and never to Bethany when it was time to select fabric and patterns. A modern store-bought dress would be a real treat. *How exciting.*

She held down her excitement, however, knowing that if she showed too much of it her aunt would likely become suspicious and might even change her mind about the dress. *Better to never show too much excitement over anything.*

She stepped into the bathroom to brush her teeth and comb out her long hair.

"When you're ready, I'll do your hair."

"Thank you, Aunt Margaret."

When Bethany came out freshened and powdered, Aunt Margaret held out Bethany's corset and said, "Turn around."

Once her aunt fit the corset around her, she turned and waited for Aunt Margaret to lace her up and then tighten the corset. Aunt Margaret tightened it, and then tightened it some more, until Bethany reached for the wall with a rising sense of panic. She was even more lightheaded than she had been at the bathhouse.

"Goodness, Aunt Margaret." She could hardly breathe. Aunt Margaret had never tied it so tight before.

Aunt Margaret yanked on the laces again and tightened the corset even more. "Uncle James wants us looking our best tonight."

So lightheaded she could hardly stand, Bethany rested her head against the wall.

"There." Aunt Margaret stood in front of her, pulled her upright, and then looked her over. "Perfect."

"You've tied it too tight."

Aunt Margaret sucked in a hiss.

Oh, no. What have I done? Daring to criticize Aunt Margaret is always a mistake.

"Small breaths. Small portions." Aunt Margaret narrowed her eyes. "If you wouldn't eat so much, you wouldn't have this problem." She turned away from

Bethany and walked across the room. "I'm not raising a little fatty."

Bethany closed her eyes, and her stomach churned. Aunt Margaret hadn't called her the nickname she hated most in a long time. She suddenly lost her appetite.

Still in a lightheaded daze, Bethany let her aunt help her into her dress, then sat on a chair while Aunt Margaret pinned up her waist length blonde hair. The pins scratched her scalp, but she barely noticed as her aunt pinned and twisted and pinned and twisted. The weight of all that hair piled upon her head, the force with which her aunt worked, and the August heat hovering in the room caused her head to ache. The headache grew worse as the heat and weight descended upon her.

When her aunt was done, Bethany remained seated. She was so hot and lightheaded, she wasn't sure she could move.

"Get up," Aunt Margaret said. "You mustn't make us late."

Bethany stood, feeling as if she were walking in a fog.

"This is a significant dinner." Aunt Margaret gave her a sharp tap on the shoulder with one finger. "I want you on your best behavior."

"Yes, ma'am."

By the way her aunt and uncle referred to it,

Bethany decided the merger must be very important to Uncle James. She would do everything she could to help. Right now, however, she stood in silence. Taking a deep breath hurt. She had no idea how she would eat.

Her aunt left her alone and went to finish getting ready. Bethany stood by the window, hoping for a breeze so she could get more air. The room was warm, and a lingering lightheadedness drew her to the fresh air. Soon it was time to go, and they headed downstairs.

Uncle James placed her hand on his arm in the elevator when she swayed as it started to move. "Time for you to eat something, young lady. I can't have my best girl wasting away."

Bethany sent him a smile she didn't feel and said nothing.

"Why, yes," Aunt Margaret said. "We can't have that."

Bethany wanted to roll her eyes but didn't. If her uncle only knew. When it came to her aunt, he only saw what he wanted to see.

The elevator opened, and they stepped out and headed for the dining room.

A well-dressed, heavyset man with brown hair and a mustache waited by the dining room door. He appeared to be near Uncle James' age. His eyes lit upon them, and he smiled.

Uncle James went up to him, urging Bethany

along with him, with Aunt Margaret on the other side.

"May I introduce my wife Margaret?"

The other man took Margaret's hand.

"Margaret, this is Mr. Richard Rivalde."

"Yes." Mr. Rivalde kissed the back of Aunt Margaret's hand. "Delighted to meet you."

"It's a pleasure to meet you at last. I've heard so much about you."

"All good, I hope."

"More than good." Aunt Margaret gave him her most charming smile.

"And this is my niece Bethany Robinson," Uncle James said.

Mr. Rivalde turned to Bethany, and his eyes widened. "Charming. My dear, you are breathtaking."

His appraising blue gaze made her stomach flip, and a wave of dizziness swept over her as he reached for her hand. Yet her manners kicked in, and she gave him a smile.

"Pleased to meet you, sir."

"The pleasure is mine." He grasped her fingertips, raised her hand to his lips, and kissed the back of it, his eyes on her face all the while. The motion seemed to take forever, and the room was much too hot.

He finally released her, but not before she noted the clamminess of his fingers. She wanted nothing more than to visit the powder room so she could wash her hands, splash water on her neck and cheeks, and loosen her tight corset. Unfortunately, the headwaiter walked over and ushered them to their table before she could excuse herself.

The table reserved for them stood in a far corner of the dining room where they would have more privacy. Once the headwaiter seated the ladies, the men took their seats.

A pianist in the corner played classical music accented by the tinkle of glasses and silverware and the muted voices of the other diners.

Bethany was dizzy, and her head felt hot and heavy. She wanted nothing more than to go upstairs, undress, and climb into her bed so everyone would leave her alone. Yet she accepted the menu the white-gloved waiter handed her and forced herself to focus on the listings.

"This is nice," Aunt Margaret said. "Mr. Rivalde, do you enjoy classical music?"

"Very much so."

"Bethany has done beautifully with her piano lessons. I do enjoy listening to her play Chopin."

"How charming." Mr. Rivalde laid his menu on the table and focused his attention on Bethany. "I would love to hear you play."

Bethany frowned. She didn't like being the center of attention. All she wanted was to find something on the menu that wouldn't make her nervous stomach even more topsy turvey.

"Bethany, Mr. Rivalde is addressing you," Aunt Margaret said in a chiding tone.

Bethany forced her frown away. "Excuse me. I was absorbed in the menu."

"What type of music is your favorite?" Mr. Rivalde again turned his strong blue gaze upon her.

She met his eyes. "My favorite type of music is jazz."

"Bethany, jazz is the devil's music. How scandalous of you. I will not have it in the house." Aunt Margaret placed her hand on her chest. "Mr. Rivalde, I assure you, she isn't serious. I don't know where she's even heard such music."

"Bethany, remember your aunt's condition," Uncle James said. "Teasing her with talk like that isn't kind."

"We didn't give you piano lessons for you to throw it all away on *jazz*." Aunt Margaret said the word as if it left a bad taste in her mouth.

Mr. Rivalde turned to Bethany. "Do you play jazz?"

"No, sir." Bethany's face heated, and she figured it had to be the color of a tomato. "I don't."

"Well," he said with a chuckle. "I can see that you like to tease your aunt. And please, there's no need for you to call me *sir*. We're all friends here, I hope."

He glanced at Uncle James. "And soon to be partners."

"Yes indeed, Richard." Uncle James beamed. "We can do away with the formalities now, I believe."

"Excellent, James."

The waiter arrived to take their order just as another waiter delivered a bottle of champagne to the next table.

"James," Aunt Margaret said. "Did you see that?"

"Yes, dear. Hot Springs is different from other parts of the country. The police turn a blind eye to drinking here."

"If you're celebrating a special occasion," the waiter said, "we can make allowances."

"Heavens, no." Shock covered Aunt Margaret's face.

"She's right. It's a bit early for our celebration," Mr. Rivalde said. "Should we change our minds, we'll let you know."

The waiter nodded and filled their water glasses.

"Prohibition is the best thing that has happened in this country. The drunkenness that goes on even now, when those who drink can be arrested... you have no idea. They should all be thrown in jail." Aunt Margaret pursed her lips for a moment, and then continued, "Some of them even show up on Sunday for church after carousing all night."

"Isn't church the best place for sinners, Aunt

Margaret?" Bethany couldn't help but speak up. "Doesn't the Bible say--"

"I'm fully behind the eighteenth amendment," Uncle James said, cutting her off. "Richard, I assure you, you won't find a drop of whiskey in my house." He harrumphed as if that were his final word.

"Good," Mr. Rivalde said. "I'm glad that Bethany hasn't been corrupted by liquor passing through her lips like so many young women her age have been."

"Bethany has always been a well behaved girl." Aunt Margaret nodded, exchanging glances with Mr. Rivalde. "A proper lady. She will make someone a fine wife. She simply needs firm direction."

"Bethany is a lovely young woman," Mr. Rivalde said. "Any man would be honored to have her by his side."

Bethany frowned. *Why must they talk about me as if I'm not here? And why is Aunt Margaret trying to play matchmaker? This is* not *good.*

"The young woman is right here, however, and able to speak for herself," Mr. Rivalde continued. "Bethany, perhaps you would like to order first."

"Oh, I--" Surprised he'd taken up for her, Bethany hesitated. She smiled at him. "Yes. Thank you, Richard. I would like the consommé, followed by the spring salad. And for the main course, I'll have the roasted chicken with a side of asparagus."

"Thank you, Miss. And for you, madam?" The waiter moved on to Aunt Margaret.

Bethany folded her hands in her lap and waited while the others ordered. For once, she would have more than half a chicken breast. *If I can stand to eat it while wearing this wretched corset. Maybe they'll let me take what's left of the chicken to the room to have later.*

Mr. Richard Rivalde was a nice man. At least he was interested in what she had to say. She sent him thoughts of thankfulness along with another smile.

He sent back a strong, confident smile of his own. *He seemed capable enough to take on anyone, even Aunt Margaret. He might prove to be a good friend.*

When dinner finally ended and they all stood in the foyer once again, Mr. Rivalde turned to Bethany.

"Would you like to attend a showing of *The Sheikh* with me? It opens here Friday night."

"Yes, I'd love to," she said. "I've been wanting to see it."

"Excellent. With your uncle's permission, of course."

"Of course you have my blessing," Uncle James said, beaming. "Richard, I'd like to discuss the merger with you tomorrow. What time is good for you?"

"A breakfast meeting suits me. I have other business to attend to later in the day."

"Very well. Breakfast it is, then."

Bethany was glad to help bring about the merger Uncle James wanted so much. *If going to a movie with Mr. Rivalde would help that along, all the better.* Aunt

Margaret hadn't raised a word against Bethany seeing the movie or going out with Mr. Rivalde. Probably because she was trying to play matchmaker.

This was working out well. Uncle James would see his merger go through. Aunt Margaret was being more pleasant than she'd been in a long time, and Bethany would get to see the movie she'd longed to see.

Hot Springs was a lovely town. Perhaps taking the baths had already improved Aunt Margaret's health, if she was being so pleasant.

With three more days until Bethany would go to the movie with Mr. Rivalde, she still had plenty of time to carry out her plan. By then, her birthday would only be a couple of days away.

CHAPTER THREE

Down the road from the Arlington hotel, Paul Tollick walked across the street. The fresh air and the walk after lunch helped him to clear his head. He crossed the open field of grass leading to the Army/Navy hospital and slowed his pace to a stroll as he topped the hill and neared the balustrade bandstand. The sticky, hot summer air made him sweat, and he lifted his hat and wiped his forehead with his handkerchief before tucking it back into his suit jacket.

A Pipevine Swallowtail butterfly flitted across his path, its blue-black coloring catching his eye and its playful flight reminding him of the summers he'd spent chasing after the delightful creatures when he was young.

He hadn't thought of butterflies in years. As a boy, he'd spent hours chasing, catching, and studying them, the wonder of examining them almost as good as the chase.

Now that little boy was long gone, and he chased criminals instead. He lived in a harsh world full of hardened criminals. Dirty deals done in back rooms, women who moved fast and stank of cigarettes and bathtub gin. Particular scents emanated from them as the evening wore on, making even the most attractive flapper seem less so the closer he got to them.

Lost in thought, Paul followed the Swallowtail butterfly.

Then he saw her.

The most beautiful woman he had ever seen sat on the steps. Her long blonde hair hung down her back in waves, telling him she'd had it pinned up recently before letting it down without combing it out. It fell to just past her waist. Her pale yellow dress blended with her hair, her pale skin, and the sun's rays to give her an almost heavenly glow.

Butterflies flitted around her as she read. She wore a wide brimmed hat and had her feet crossed at the ankles in a ladylike pose. Slowing his steps and taking in every detail, he blinked twice to make sure she was real. The desire to look into her eyes and hear her voice led him on until he stood in front of her.

"Pardon me, miss."

She looked up at him, and he discovered her

wide blue eyes were the same color as the butterfly he'd followed. She had a perfect nose and soft, pink lips, and didn't have a trace of makeup upon her beautiful face. She took his breath away.

"Yes?"

"May I sit?" He gestured to the bench where she sat.

She blinked once as if unsure she should allow it, and then looked away. "Of course."

"Thank you. This is a good spot to rest."

"Yes, it is." She gathered herself slowly, as if she'd been lost in another world. The world of her book, perhaps. She shifted over.

He sat beside her. "I didn't mean to disturb your reading."

"Oh, no. It's fine. I don't mind."

"My name is Paul. Paul Tollick."

"Pleased to meet you, Paul. I'm Bethany Robinson."

"The pleasure is mine."

She smiled and dipped her hat to hide her soft smile.

"What are you reading?"

"Stoddard's lectures." Placing her bookmark inside, she closed the maroon leather bound book and showed him the spine.

"Constantinople/Jerusalem/Egypt." He read the gold lettering aloud as she sat smiling at him. "You enjoy reading about foreign places?"

"Yes." Her breathy voice came out shy as a whisper. "I plan to read my way through all of them. I've been reading them in between my regular studies for a year now."

"May I?" He held out his hand for the book, and she gave it him. Flipping the book open to the page she had marked, he took in a picture of Turkish officers smoking pipes outside the Galata Café. "Interesting."

"Yes," she answered in a soft voice. "I think so."

He continued flipping pages, noting the Mosque of Suleiman and the Golden Horn, including the water beyond it, men wearing turbans, more mosques and Turkish baths, the sultan's palace, a gypsy camp. He stopped at the description of a harem.

What did this innocent young woman know or wish to know of harems? For he couldn't mistake the innocence shining from her eyes. The trust, the purity, the glow.

"This interests you?" He searched her eyes looking for answers to his questions about this beautiful, intriguing woman.

"Oh, yes." She blushed and bit her lip, then looked down at her hands clasped in her lap, her hat hiding her face.

"The word *harem*," he read aloud, "means sacred enclosure. A place secure from all intrusion."

She returned her gaze to him, taking in each word, the blush still covering her cheeks.

"Is this what interests you? The security? Like a convent might be?" He had to know what lit up her face like that, what drew her to read about that exotic place.

"Oh, no." She shook her head. "I'd never want to be locked away from the world again."

Again. So she'd once been locked away or had at least felt as if she had been.

"Again?" He held out the book, and she clasped it with both hands as if she needed something to hold on to, and then pressed it to her chest without speaking.

"Forgive me. I'm intruding. You barely know me."

"I-I didn't mean anything by that. No one's... no one's ever locked me up."

She wasn't being entirely truthful, and her lie was so clear upon her face it could have been drawn there with a fountain pen. *Perhaps she hadn't been locked up, but she believed she'd been. Interesting.* He was so accustomed to interrogating born liars and catching their tells that her blatant honesty, combined with the way she tried to lie, made him want to smile.

He glanced away from her and focused on the dancing butterflies, the blue of their wings reminding him of her eyes.

Bethany. Even her name was light and delicate, like a butterfly.

She swallowed and nervousness radiated from of her, much like the butterflies flitting about, unsure where to land.

Remembering how one caught a butterfly, he sat quietly for a moment. Then just before the air between them became too uncomfortable, he met her eyes.

"Pipe-vine Swallowtail."

"What?" Confusion filled her blue eyes, but he turned to face the butterflies and watched her from his peripheral vision.

"The butterflies."

"Oh." She breathed in, wonder in her voice as she watched them with him. "They are beautiful."

"Yes, they are." *Like you.* Blue wings flitting in the air, catching sunlight.

They sat in companionable silence for several more minutes watching the butterflies, until he sensed she'd relaxed just a bit.

"I used to collect butterflies when I was a boy."

"You did?" She turned to him again, but he kept his gaze upon the Swallowtails flitting about.

"Yes." He smiled. "I did. I've never told anyone that before." He turned to look at her. "Will you keep my secret? No telling what others might think if they find out this detective's interested in butterflies. I'd never hear the end of it."

"Oh, I promise." Her lovely blue eyes were wide now, sincere in her promise. "I'll never tell a soul."

"Good." Somehow he knew she wouldn't.

She kept her gaze on him and curiosity filled her features. "You're a detective?"

"Yes, ma'am. The Real McCoy."

"The Real McCoy?"

"Bona fide."

"Goodness." She blinked twice as she took it in. "Are you here on vacation, or are you chasing bad men?"

"I'm..." He hesitated and let the word trail off, unwilling to tell her who he was chasing or why. "I'm here on unofficial-official business, so technically I'm on vacation. And you?"

"I'm here with my aunt and uncle, who came for the baths."

"Have you seen much of the town yet?"

"No, we only arrived the day before yesterday."

"Well I hope you enjoy your stay." He reached into his pocket. "I was just about to have a candy bar. Would you like half of a Baby Ruth?"

"Oh. Yes, thank you."

He broke the Baby Ruth in half, peeled down the wrapper, and held it out.

She took it, held it with two fingers, and ate it as delicately as he'd ever seen anyone eat anything. Then she licked melted chocolate off each finger, closing her eyes as she savored the taste. Pure enjoyment filled her features.

He held back a groan.

She had no idea the affect her pink tongue licking her fingertips had on him. Half of him wanted to protect her and hide her away from any man who might touch her, and the other half wanted to be the man touching her, making her close her eyes and watching her expression as he introduced her to the art of lovemaking.

He shifted, and she opened her eyes to look at him again.

"That was so good," she said. "Thank you. I'm not allowed to have candy bars."

"What?" He frowned. "You're not *allowed* to have candy bars?"

"My aunt keeps a close watch on my figure. She always thinks I'm gaining weight and getting fat."

He took in her round, full breasts, her small waist, and her rounded hips. She didn't have the slim figure of a cigarette smoking, gin-drinking flapper, but he very much admired and preferred her curvy shape. *She was far from fat.*

"You're perfect just as you are. Not fat, and not too thin."

"Still, she thinks I'm fat," Bethany said with a shrug. "She controls what food I eat and how much, so I don't have any choice."

"Why do you let her control what you eat?"

"She won't be able to soon. I'll be eighteen on Sunday."

He leaned back and studied her. God help him, she was even younger than he'd thought. No, he'd wanted to believe she was older, despite her youthful beauty that should have told him she was young, possibly underage.

He'd just given an underage girl a candy bar in the park. Forget telling anyone about his interest in butterflies. *This was worse.* He now looked like a dirty old man. Even though he wasn't even ten years older than she, and many women married older men, he still wanted to shake himself. *This was not acceptable behavior. Not acceptable behavior for him.*

"Well, I'd best be going." He stood. "I enjoyed meeting you, Bethany."

"I'm--" She stood too, clutching her book and blushing. She faltered. "I'm free every day at one o'clock when my aunt takes her treatment." Her big blue eyes met his. "If you want to watch butterflies again, it can be our secret."

With her eyes gazing into his in that way, he couldn't tell her no, even if someone had a gun pointed at his head. He couldn't tell her yes, either. He needed time to think things through.

"Perhaps. Now, don't take any more candy from strangers."

"Oh." She gasped, as if only now realizing what she'd done. "No, I won't do that again. I promise."

Suddenly her smile turned bright. "But we aren't strangers anymore. We're friends."

Beautiful Bethany. So naïve, blind, and trusting. Fragile as a butterfly. He wanted to shake some street sense into her. To hold her close and protect her, so she'd never need it.

The butterflies had flown away, and that told him the time had come for him to go. *Time for her to go back to her safe life with her aunt and uncle.*

"Yes, I'm your friend. If you're ever in trouble, call me." He wasn't sure telling her that was the wisest thing to do. Yet they were in Hot Springs, a town full of gangsters, and he wanted to be sure she stayed safe. "You can reach me at the Hotel Arlington."

"Oh, you're staying there, too?" She beamed up at him. "That's our hotel."

"You're staying at the Arlington?" Paul gaped at her as the information sank in.

She nodded and smiled a smile bright as the sun.

"Stay away from the fourth floor, Bethany," he said in a stern tone, aware she needed to know and pay attention to what he said.

"Why?" She crinkled her nose, and that made her look adorable.

"You've heard of Al Capone?"

She shook her head no.

Of course she hadn't. Where'd she been living? Under a rock? Off in some convent? What was the best way to explain who Capone was without making her too interested in him?

"He's a very dangerous man... *the Big Cheese*. The fourth floor is full of dangerous men."

"Are those men the reason you're here?" Her eyes widened. "Are you going to arrest them?"

"No, not arrest them. I'm going to watch them and find out who their associates are while they're here. Back room deals are made in this town. I want you to stay far away from them. And if you see me at the Arlington, don't wave or come over and talk to me. Also, don't talk to anyone else about this."

"Well, all right." She agreed but appeared perplexed. He wondered what was going through her pretty blonde head.

"Bethany, I really have to go now. If you need me, call." Why was he having so much trouble pulling himself away when he knew it was the right thing to do?

"Okay, I will. I hope to see you later. I have something to do tomorrow, but I might be able to come to the park afterward for a little while if it doesn't take too long. After that, I can come here at the same time every day. My aunt takes her treatments every day at one. Will I see you tomorrow?"

"Maybe." He gave her a smile. "Stay safe, Bethany Robinson."

"Of course."

He turned, held up his hand in a goodbye wave

and headed away from her, toward the hotel where he would find a spot to watch her and make sure she made it back safe.

A national park policeman wearing a blue-serge uniform with brass buttons walked past him, making his rounds just like clockwork. *Hot Springs might be crooked, but the police did their best to maintain order.* That made it the perfect place for Paul to watch certain men and see who kept company with them. *At least here, unlike in Chicago, the crooks laid down their big guns and didn't shoot each other in a fight over territory. Bethany would be safe as long as she stayed out of their way. She could vacation here with her family and then go back home.*

Paul was here to gather information, report back to his superiors, and help build a case that would hold up in court. He was one of the newer detectives on the case, so none of Al Capone's men should recognize him.

That was why his boss had sent him here. Because he could stay in the background, unnoticed. As long as Bethany didn't blow his cover.

EVERY TIME BETHANY had looked up into Paul Tollick's deep brown eyes, she'd been pinned in place, unable to move a muscle. When he had asked if he could sit with her, her heart had gone all aflutter. Goodness, but he was handsome. He had to be at least six feet tall, and whenever he smiled, the motion warmed her all the way down to her toes.

Paul finally walked away, and Bethany felt as if the sun had gone back behind the clouds. She wanted to run after him, to call him back. He moved with strong, quiet grace. He was so alive, so strong, and so handsome, and he made her feel beautiful.

Did he carry a gun? Surely he must, since he was a detective.

Oh, I should have asked him.

She hadn't, because she didn't know how to talk to boys. Bethany had only been on one date two years ago, a date that hadn't gone well. Uncle James had flung open the front door and yelled at the boy for bringing her home late and then trying to kiss her on the front porch.

Poor Clarence.

After that, Aunt Margaret had announced that Bethany would not go on any more dates unless Uncle James met the boys first and gave them his approval.

Bethany had given up. No other boys would ask her out, anyway. She didn't go to the local school because Aunt Margaret believed public school encouraged wild behavior. No, her aunt hired tutors to teach Bethany, the same way she had been taught. If Bethany hadn't met Clarence at the drug store in town, she wouldn't have gone out on a date with him, either.

She spent her free time reading about exotic places all over the world and dreaming of having adventures. About Egypt and Turkey and sheiks and harems. She wasn't studying the book because of the section on Jerusalem like she'd told her aunt. The only book Aunt Margaret ever read was the Bible, so she would never figure out what Bethany was really reading about.

As Paul walked away, Bethany wished he were the one taking her to see *The Son of the Sheik* at the movie theater instead of Mr. Rivalde. Her aunt and uncle would never give her their permission to go out with Paul. With all the rules she had to live under, she might as well live in a prison or a cage, like a trapped butterfly.

Once she turned eighteen, she'd be able to do what she wanted.

Richard Rivalde now seemed much too old for her. She wished she hadn't said yes to the movie, but she'd wanted to see the show and this might be her only chance to do so.

On her walk to back to the hotel, she couldn't think of anything but Paul and how she wished *he* were taking her to see the show.

Of how she hoped to see him again tomorrow.

CHAPTER FOUR

"Bethany, are you listening to me?"

"Yes, Aunt Margaret, I'm listening." Bethany lounged across the bed slowly flipping the pages of her book as she read the next section in Stoddard's Lectures.

"Dr. Frederick says you would benefit from another treatment. When you go with me today, they can fit you in." She sniffed. "It will be much better than you wandering about the hill getting a sunburn as you did yesterday."

"It's just a bit of pink in my cheeks, not a sunburn."

"Still, I don't want you wandering about."

"I'm not up to all that heat today. The hot water will make me feel dizzy." Before her aunt could respond, Bethany hurried to say, "I promise not to leave the hotel today."

Surprise crossed Aunt Margaret's face.

Bethany forced a yawn. "I might even take a nap."

"I'll tell James not to disturb you."

"Thank you." Bethany went back to her book.

Aunt Margaret watched her for a moment, and then turned away to get ready.

Bethany had a hard time pretending to be sleepy and keeping down the excitement and anticipation about what she planned to do today. She hadn't been truthful with her aunt, and that bothered her. *Aunt Margaret bent the truth all the time to get what she wanted, so it didn't seem as awful as being dishonest with someone else would have. Still...*

Aunt Margaret fussed about, taking a long time to get ready, as usual. Time dragged as sunbeams poured in through the window, heating the room. Bethany watched her aunt out of the corner of her eye instead of reading as she pretended to do. Fussing over her hair when she was just going to take off her clothes and get into a steamy bath or sauna didn't make any sense, did it? If only her aunt would hurry up.

She kept watching Bethany as she fussed in the mirror. "Are you sure you don't feel up to a treatment?"

"Yes, ma'am."

"Well, all right, then." Finally, after casting one

last look at Bethany, Aunt Margaret left to walk to her appointment at The Fordyce.

Bethany closed her book and hurried to the window, staying back so Aunt Margaret wouldn't see her. Several long minutes passed until finally, her aunt disappeared around the corner. Excited to finally put her plan in motion and happy to be free, Bethany ran to her suitcase to retrieve the money she'd saved. She hadn't spent a dime over the past few months while saving up for the most daring thing she'd ever done in her life.

She was going to have her hair cut in the latest fashion so she wouldn't be such an odd duck. Briefly she thought of Paul and wondered if he'd think she was pretty once she'd cut her hair. Then she pushed the thought aside.

Placing her money into her purse, she went out the door and locked it behind her. A maid came out of one of the rooms and walked down the hallway carrying a food tray while Bethany waited for the elevator. She smiled at the woman. A combination of excitement and nerves filled her, but from the way the maid returned her smile only her happy anticipation must have shown.

Bethany rode the elevator down to the beauty shop at the basement level of the hotel. Women shoppers moved down the hallway and slipped in and out of the stores. Bethany spotted a dress shop, a shoe store, and a store that sold everything from postcards to toothpaste.

She paused at the window of the beauty shop. Several stylish beauticians moved about inside, each with their hair in a tight bob, the latest most popular hairdo.

All girls wore their hair that way now. Bethany stood out among others her age with her old fashioned hair and her long dresses, and she'd decided the time had come for that to stop.

She squared her shoulders and walked inside. The women turned to look at her. Bethany touched her hand to the back of her pinned up hair.

"I'd like a haircut, please."

"Sure, doll." The dark haired woman leaning upon the wooden counter which held the black and gold cash register turned and snuffed out her cigarette in a cut glass cigarette dish. "What do ya have in mind?"

"Well..." Bethany hesitated. "I want it shorter." She squared her shoulders again and stood up straight. "*Much* shorter."

"I know just the thing." A knowing look entered the woman's eyes as she took in Bethany's pinned up blonde hair. She pointed toward a chair in front of one of the mirrors. "Have a seat and let's see what you've got."

Bethany sat on the chair the beautician indicted.

"I'm Tildy." The woman draped a cloth around

Bethany's shoulders and leaned in to whisper, "That's short for Matilda, a name I don't answer to."

"I'm Bethany."

"All right, doll," Tildy picked up a comb and stood behind Bethany. "Do you want to take it down, or do you want me to do it?"

Bethany reached for the pins holding her waist long hair. Tildy watched her for a moment before putting down the comb and helping her to remove the pins, hurrying the process along.

Soon Bethany's golden tresses fell down over her shoulders and back. Tildy lifted the long blonde hair and ran her fingers through it. "This hair looks like it has never been cut."

"Today will be my first haircut." Bethany took a deep breath and looked into the mirror. *Aunt Margaret will have a fit when she sees I've cut my hair, but once it's done she can't do a thing about it.*

Tildy met her eyes in the mirror. "How short do you want it?"

"Shoulder length."

"To here?" Tildy placed a hand on Bethany's shoulder.

"A little higher."

Tildy raised her hand until it hovered just above Bethany's shoulders and near her chin.

Bethany nodded.

"You're sure?" Tildy stood holding her hair. "Once I cut it, there's no going back."

"I'm sure." Bethany smiled.

Tildy reached for her scissors, and Bethany closed her eyes. *I can't watch.*

Snip.

Bethany caught her breath. *I'm really doing this.*

Tildy kept snipping, and soon Bethany's head felt much lighter. Maybe her headaches would stop now. She was so tired of the headaches and of her aunt fussing over her, only making them worse.

"Do you want bangs?"

"No." Bethany's eyes flew open. That might feel strange. She wasn't used to having hair above her eyes and wasn't sure when she'd save enough money to have her hair cut again after it grew out. Or even where she could go to have it cut once she was back home. Or how to get away from the house long enough to do it. Squirreling away enough for this haircut had taken months, and if not for the treatments Aunt Margaret took every day, Bethany wouldn't have been able to have it cut today.

Her eyes widened as she looked at herself in the mirror. Her hair now had a natural wave. *Who would've thought? Where had the waviness come from?* Her hair had always been long and straight.

Soft blonde waves framed her face and made her eyes appear wider.

Tildy fluffed the bottom of Bethany's hair with both hands. "Many gals would kill for the natural waves you have, doll."

She nodded.

"You won't need to do a thing to it unless you want a Marcel wave."

"No, I don't want one of those. I can't believe my hair has a natural wave. That's amazing." She didn't have enough money to buy the Marcel curling iron. Besides, Aunt Margaret would only take the iron away. She'd be angry enough because Bethany had cut her hair.

Bethany loved her new haircut.

She turned her head from side to side and enjoyed the swish of her hair. A slow grin spread across her face. She felt sassy. New. Bolder.

"I like it," she said.

"Good. That'll be five dollars."

Bethany opened her coin purse and counted out the money. She had just enough left to treat herself to a Yahoo tomorrow, if Aunt Margaret would let her leave the hotel room. She could very well end up locked in the room for the rest of their trip.

Yet she didn't care. Her new haircut was worth whatever her aunt might do.

Besides, Aunt Margaret could only lock her up until her birthday.

PAUL TOLLICK COULDN'T BELIEVE his eyes. *Was that Bethany walking across the lobby?*

She'd cut her hair.

So that was why she hadn't been in her usual spot today. She'd planned this. The haircut was why she'd said she might be late.

She paused to take a drink from the drinking fountain. He moved closer, as if waiting to take a drink, all the while taking in the people around him.

She stood and wiped the back of her hand across her lips. Then she saw him, and her blue eyes widened. Her whole face lit up. "Oh, Paul."

"Bethany." A slow smile spread across his face. He cupped the bottom of her hair and fluffed it as his gaze roamed from her eyes, to her face, and then back to her hair.

She didn't move.

"I like it," he said. "It's much more touchable." His smile deepened. "And so soft."

She blushed.

"It looks good on you."

"Thank you." She paused. "My aunt will have a fit when she sees me. I might not be at the park tomorrow if she gets angry."

Nervousness and uncertainty about what she'd done filled her eyes. The nervousness flitted over every inch of her skin, reminding him of the flitting, fragile wings of a butterfly. *She seemed so young. Had she never gone against her aunt's wishes before? Never stood up to her?*

"You're old enough to wear your hair however

you like. It's your hair, not hers." He cocked his head to reappraise her new haircut as more uncertainty and even a bit of fear came into her eyes. "I love it."

Her sudden smile could have lit up the ballroom of the hotel. He hoped to see more of that smile and less of the uncertainty.

Breathlessly she asked, "You do?"

"Yes, Bethany. I do."

"I'm glad." She gazed up at him, and he thought of kissing her. Doing so had been on his mind since he'd first met her yesterday, but the hotel lobby wasn't the place to kiss young women, especially those not yet of age with restrictive guardians. *She deserved soft, lingering kisses beneath an arbor, not kisses stolen in dark corners of a hotel, however grand.*

He wasn't in the habit of stealing kisses or anything else from women. He took nothing they didn't freely give. Women offered themselves to him more and more, the jazz and bathtub gin creating a boldness he now realized he'd grown accustomed to experiencing.

Bethany, the complete opposite of those women, needed to be wooed and won. No, she deserved to be wooed and adored. He would enjoy every minute of wooing her.

He enjoyed having her near. *It was that simple.*

"I thought you didn't want me to speak to you here." Her blue eyes showed her confusion, and she kept her voice so low he had to lean forward to hear her.

He gave her a slight smile. "Yes, I know. We'd best go before we attract attention."

Despite telling her to act as if she didn't know him if she saw him at the hotel, he'd been drawn to approach her. She was too young, and in her naiveté could cause problems with his ability to go unnoticed, and yet he'd still gone against his own advice. He simply couldn't stay away from her. No other woman had ever affected him like this, and that worried him. *She could mean trouble...* and when it came to his job, he couldn't afford trouble.

"Tomorrow in the park?" Her soft voice struck him as unsure.

He bent down to take a drink of water from the water fountain while pretending to ignore her. "Perhaps. Now go."

"Goodbye," she whispered, confusion pouring off her in waves.

He didn't answer but continued to drink as she walked away.

"WHAT HAVE YOU DONE?" Aunt Margaret's eyes darkened to black slits the moment they landed on Bethany. Anger radiated off her like heat from a boiling furnace. She slammed the door. "You little fool."

Bethany widened her eyes. She'd never seen her aunt this angry. Her fury froze whatever words Bethany might have spoken. She wanted to run and hide as she had when she was a small girl, yet she wasn't that small girl anymore and she had nowhere to hide, anyway. She never had.

"You gave your word you wouldn't leave this hotel."

"I didn't leave the hotel. They have a beauty parlor right here in the basement."

"I cannot leave you alone for even one minute." Aunt Margaret's face was a mask of fury. "You cannot be trusted."

"I kept my word. I didn't leave the hotel."

"You are a disgrace. You have disgraced this family. How do you expect to go out in society? That hairdo is unladylike. We won't find you a proper husband with you looking like that. If you were married, it would be grounds for divorce. You're a fool."

"I like it, and I'm not the only one. Others have told me it looks pretty."

"Of course the beautician who cut your hair is going to tell you that. People like that will tell you anything when they want to sell you something. Not only is your haircut unladylike, it makes your face look fat."

Bethany's stomach clenched. She wasn't fat. She wasn't. Paul thought she looked pretty. She'd known her aunt would be angry, but hadn't known she'd be *this* angry. If only Bethany could flee. *Anywhere but inside this room. Anywhere far away from her aunt.*

"You'll be lucky if Richard still wants to take you to that movie." Her aunt paced the room. "Just wait until your uncle sees."

"Sees what?" Uncle James stepped through the door, and his jaw dropped. He didn't even close the door behind him as he walked into the room.

Bethany reached up to the back of her hair and fluffed it as Tildy and Paul had done. That felt good, although she knew her aunt and uncle might take it as a defiant move. *Paul likes my hair this way. I like it too. I don't care what they think.*

"You've cut your hair," Uncle James said. He wasn't usually one to state the obvious, and yet he seemed dumbfounded.

She nodded. "Yes, I did."

"Well." He slammed the door. "It's done now."

Bethany smiled at him rather than responding. A silent smile had always been her best way of responding to Uncle James. He didn't like for her to speak out of turn or to talk back. At least he hadn't yelled or acted as if it were the end of the world the way her aunt had.

"It certainly is. I told her she'll be lucky if Richard doesn't change his mind about taking her to the movie." Aunt Margaret scowled. "It's positively indecent."

"Richard isn't a man to go back on his word." Uncle James frowned. "Though whether he'll ask her again..."

"Yes, exactly. He's expecting a lovely, well bred girl, not a misbehaving girl who won't listen." Aunt Margaret turned to face Bethany again. "You'll do everything possible to be pleasant to Mr. Robinson so he won't regret asking you. Let's just hope he isn't embarrassed to be seen with you now."

"Hair grows out," Uncle James said. He placed a hand on Aunt Margaret's shoulder. "And I see no danger of the merger falling through. Our meeting today was most agreeable."

"Well, goodness. I'm glad the merger hasn't fallen through. Though I don't see what my hair has to do with that," Bethany said.

Her aunt and uncle exchanged glances but didn't answer her.

"Get ready for dinner," Uncle James said. "It's done. I see no reason to discuss it any more. Bethany Marie, I expect no further surprises from you. Do you understand?"

"Yes, sir." She wouldn't give them any more surprises.

Once my birthday comes, I'll tell Uncle James about my plans and he'll explain my inheritance so I'll know how to proceed. Unlike Aunt Margaret, he's always been honest with me. He deserves the same consideration.

They dressed for dinner in silence. Uncle James called down to request a private dining area so her aunt would be less embarrassed to be seen with Bethany.

CHAPTER FIVE

ncle James arranged for Bethany to visit the library the following day. She'd finished her book and wanted something new to read.

Aunt Margaret pursed her lips but reluctantly agreed when Uncle James said the librarian would keep an eye on Bethany. Reading had always kept Bethany out of trouble as a small child, and the library was a safe place where no harm would befall her.

Bethany waited all of thirty minutes before taking a lunch break and heading back to the Arlington. Her aunt and uncle hadn't taken into account that the library didn't serve lunch, and she decided that a lunch break was a reasonable reason to leave her spot beneath the watchful eyes of the librarian. Neither did they know the librarian Uncle

James had introduced her to would also take a lunch break, so a different librarian would be in her place for a time. One who hadn't yet met Bethany. *Really,* Bethany thought as she walked away. *A librarian isn't a chaperone. Nor am I a child who needs someone to watch over me.*

At the Arlington, she went down to the basement and looked at the dresses in the window of the dress shop. Her gaze lit upon a pale blue dress.

"That one would look good on you," a friendly voice said.

Bethany turned to meet the eyes of a stunning flapper who stood next to her. The woman's jet-black hair was cut in a bob that framed her face just so. She also had smoky eyes and a beauty mark beside her lips that marked her as one of the more fashionable set. *She could have been a movie star, she was so pretty.*

"I don't have the money for that dress or any other," Bethany replied. "I spent all my money on my new haircut. The first haircut I've ever had."

"So that's why you're wearing such a dowdy old dress." The woman swept her gaze over Bethany from head to toe and back up again. "You've started a metamorphosis you can't finish."

Self-consciousness came over Bethany, and her face fell. Her new haircut didn't matter. She'd still never fit in.

"Don't be so sad, doll face." The woman laughed.

"I can fix you up. Your hair looks good. You could be a stunner. You just need a little help. I'm Suki." Suki stuck out her hand.

Bethany smiled, reached out, and shook it. "I'm Bethany."

"Whoa, that's an old fashioned name. We'll work on that. Come on up to my room," Suki said. "I'll get you fixed up in a jiff. A dress, some makeup, the works. We'll put on our glad rags, and you'll be ready to hit the town."

"Oh gosh, Suki, that'll be wonderful. Thank you." Suki was so nice to do this for a complete stranger she'd just met. Bethany followed her to the elevator.

The woman laughed. "Anytime. I've got more clothes than I need. I only have to ask for what I want, cause my sugar daddy's real good to me."

The elevator opened, and they stepped inside. Suki pushed the elevator button for four.

Four. Oh, no. I promised Paul I'd stay away from the fourth floor.

"You're on four?"

"Why, yes. I am. That's why I pressed it."

What should I do? Suki seems so nice. I don't want to hurt her feelings by telling her I can't go to her room.

Lost in thought, Bethany didn't reply. She stood frowning at the number four on the elevator panel.

"Don't worry, doll, I have just the thing. You'll be all dolled up in no time." Suki tapped the toe of her shoe on the elevator floor with impatience. "These elevators are so slow."

When the door opened, Suki rushed out and reached into her purse for her key. Bethany followed along behind her and looked about.

The fourth floor didn't look any different from the fifth floor, except for the man in the dark suit sitting in a chair at the end of the hall. *He didn't look dangerous.*

When Suki unlocked the door to her room, Bethany followed her in, closed the door behind her, and gasped in amazement.

Dresses and hats were flung everywhere. Boas, feathers, and shoes were scattered about, and empty bottles of champagne sat on every surface.

Suki grasped Bethany by the hand, pulled her over to a wardrobe, and flung it open. Dresses in more colors than Bethany could count hung inside.

"Oh, they're all so pretty."

"First, though," Suki said, still holding her hand and swinging it as if they were schoolgirls. "Your old things have to go."

Bethany almost giggled, and a giddiness rose up within her thanks to this new friend and her soon to be achieved freedom.

Suki helped Bethany out of her dress and then her slip. Her corset, hose, and panties were all that remained.

"Turn around," Suki said.

Bethany turned and faced a full-length mirror as the other woman reached for something on the dresser.

Snip. Snip. Snip.

The back of her corset pulled apart on each side, and the cold steel of the scissors met her back. She shivered, and goose bumps broke out across her skin. When the corset dropped, she caught it and held it, her cheeks heating as her breasts bobbed and her nipples pebbled. Embarrassment washed over her.

Seeming unaffected by Bethany's semi-nudity, Suki whisked the corset out of her hands.

"We can burn this thing, if you like," she said. "Some women do."

"Oh, no. I wouldn't want to start a fire." Bethany cupped her breasts in an effort to maintain her modesty, but even the touch of her hands felt naughty somehow.

"Always the good girl, aren't you?" One corner of Suki's mouth turned up in a mischievous grin.

"Well, I--" Bethany frowned and looked down at her feet. "I guess."

The thud of what must have been her corset hitting the metal trashcan behind her startled her, but she didn't look up. A bone deep shyness had come over her.

"Take a deep breath," Suki said. "You're free now."

Bethany took a breath and then let it out.

"That wasn't very deep." Suki placed her hands on Bethany's waist. "Your waist is so small. Almost too small, from wearing those corsets. Whoever invented them should be shot. A woman can't breathe in one of those things. She can't move much, and she sure as hell isn't free. Doesn't this feel better already?" She moved her hands up to touch the bottom of Bethany's ribs. "You can expand more here, take a breath, and really *breathe.*"

"Yes, I guess."

"Seriously." Suki stilled her hands. "Take a deep breath. I mean it. I want to show you something."

Bethany took a breath.

"Not like that. That's a little breath. I want you to fill your lungs all the way down to here." Suki touched Bethany's rib cage where she wanted Bethany to breathe in deep. "Push your ribcage out to the side as it expands when you breathe in. Push against my hands."

Bethany took a deep breath. Doing so was harder than it sounded.

"More."

She breathed deeper, and the bottom of her rib cage moved out a little more.

"That's it. Feel how your ribs press against my hands. Take more deep breaths like that."

After Bethany practiced a few more minutes of deep breathing, Suki released her.

"Now you've got it. Let go and keep breathing deep. It's good for you. Will make you feel like a new woman."

Breathing deeply really did feel wonderful. Different, but good. A slow smile spread across Bethany's face.

"Better?" Suki perched on the arm of a chair and reached for a cigarette.

"Yes. *Much* better."

"Good." Placing the cigarette in a long silver holder, Suki reached for a lighter and flicked it. She lit the cigarette and then inhaled. "Ciggy?"

"No, thank you. I don't smoke."

Silence hovered for a moment. Finally, Suki said, "Are you embarrassed by your breasts?"

"Oh. Well, no. I guess not." Bethany dropped her hands to her sides. "It's just that no one but my aunt and my doctor have ever seen them. I'm not used to anyone looking at them."

"They're quite big for someone with your small frame."

"Yes, my aunt took me to the doctor about it when I was younger." Bethany wanted to cover up again but didn't. Suki was being so matter of fact about everything, covering herself up seemed childish. "She even asked the doctor about them, but he said they were perfectly normal and they just kept growing."

"Oh, they're perfect. Perfect, round, and melonlike." Suki inhaled again, and then blew out a line of smoke. "I've never seen any so peachy perfect."

"Have you seen many?"

"Sure, doll. If you go to petting parties, you're bound to see them." She laughed.

Puzzled by what was so funny, Bethany stared at her. What was a petting party?

"We'll have to bind you."

"Bind me?" That sounded alarming and painful. Something she wouldn't like at all.

"Your breasts, doll face. They're not in fashion, so we'll have to bind them. Too much jiggle, you know." Suki laughed. "Give one of your shoulders a shake, and you'll see." She jiggled her shoulders in a shoulder shimmy to demonstrate. "Try it."

Bethany imitated the movement, and her breasts jiggled. Widening her eyes, she reached to cover them again.

Suki laughed so hard *her* shoulders shook. "Can you imagine how much they'd bounce if you did the Charleston or the shimmy? Honey, when you shimmy, you're still going to have plenty of shaking going on. Yet if they're bound, you won't put out anyone's eye."

Bethany giggled, and everything jiggled again. Her laughter wouldn't stop. Standing here in a room with a girlfriend sharing secrets and laughter felt so *good.* Looking forward to more good times, standing nearly nude didn't bother her nearly as much as she had feared.

Suki found a roll of white gauze in the dresser drawer and wrapped it around Bethany's breasts, binding them to her chest. Doing so still wouldn't produce the boyish, flat chested look so many girls had, but at least it would help her contain the jiggle. In addition, without the binding, her breasts would remain bare beneath her dress like Suki's. Bethany wasn't ready for that. Still, she had so much more freedom of movement with the gauze than with the corset.

Bethany decided she hated corsets. She would never wear one again.

The dress Suki pulled out was a heavily beaded, golden fabric with gold beading, thin straps, and a drop waist. "You can have this one. I never wear it anymore, and it's the perfect color with your hair."

"Thank you." Slipping the soft, slinky dress over her head, Bethany adjusted it around her hips and looked in the mirror. A modern, pale skinned, blonde haired flapper looked back at her. The golden dress reminded her of the golden glow the sun sent through the stained glass windows at the Fordyce Bathhouse. *It was so lovely.* Warmth and happiness spread through her as if she'd been sitting beneath that golden glow, and she smiled.

Suki adjusted the dress at Bethany's hips. "Your hips are almost too curvy for this. We can't do anything about it, though. It'll do." She stepped back. "You need either a cloche hat or a beaded headband to match."

"Yes. All of my hats are too big."

"Too old fashioned, you mean. That's what happens when you let an old bluenose pick out your clothes."

"True." Those days were over now for Bethany. In just a few days, she would be of age and would ask her uncle to go over the details of her inheritance line by line. Soon she'd pick out her own clothes and wear whatever she liked.

Suki paused with her hand on her hip surveying Bethany from head to toe. "Golden from head to toe. That color really does suit you, but now you need a splash of color. Where's your lipstick?"

"I don't have any. I'm not allowed to wear it."

Suki raised an eyebrow. "Really?"

"That's the truth."

"Well, I can fix that in a jiffy." She went the bathroom and rummaged through a travel case filled with makeup. "Red. Every woman should at least have one tube. Men love it when a woman wears red." She emerged from the bathroom holding a lipstick tube out to Bethany. "This is the ticket."

"I don't know." Filled with uncertainty about the bold color, Bethany took it from her and opened the lid. "It's very red."

"Go on," Suki waved her toward the bathroom mirror. "Try it out."

Bethany went into the bathroom and applied the lipstick to her lips, then stared at herself.

The red stood out against her pale complexion. "I don't know Suki. It's very bright."

"Let me see." Suki came up behind her. "Doll face, it's perfect. You have the perfect little bow shaped mouth. Men will line up to kiss you."

Bethany blushed and giggled as she imaged all sorts of men lining up to kiss her. Her lack of kissing experience embarrassed her. It was about time she did something about it. She wondered what Paul's kisses would taste like and how they would feel.

"You can keep that one," Suki gestured to the tube of lipstick. "I have others."

"Thank you."

"I can't give you any stockings because I've ruined all mine and need to buy some new ones, but you'll need a different kind anyway."

"Suki, you've already done so much."

"Not so much," Suki shrugged. "Now listen, doll. The latest fashion is to roll your stockings down to your knee."

"Oh." That took Bethany by surprise. "How do they stay up without a garter belt?"

"Sometimes they don't." Suki laughed. "Some of us even roll them down *below* the knee. You'll see when we go dancing."

"I can't wait to learn all the dances."

"I can teach you. Right now, though," Suki reached into the back of the wardrobe and pulled out a silver flask. "It's time to celebrate your freedom."

"Oh, I don't know." Bethany had never had a drop of alcohol touch her lips.

Suki drew her brows together. "Don't be a wet blanket, doll."

Still unsure, Bethany changed her mind and decided to try it. How would she know if she did or didn't like it unless she tasted it? *Plenty of people had drunk communion wine before prohibition went through.* She even remembered her mama and daddy drinking wine once at a birthday dinner for her mama. Before they'd both died in a car accident. *All of the adults had laughed and enjoyed themselves drinking toasts and dancing.* She didn't see anything wrong with drinking. She just couldn't let her aunt and uncle know.

"All right." She was ready to taste it. She was ready to try a lot of things. Like riding a bicycle and driving a car. All of the things other girls did that Aunt Margaret and Uncle James wouldn't allow Bethany to do. "I'll try it."

"Now you're on the trolley." Suki handed her the silver flask that had an *S* engraved on the front.

Raising it to her lips, Bethany took a small sip of the liquid inside. It tasted strong and a little sweet, although not sweet enough to lessen its kick. She swallowed, blinked, and coughed. Then she handed the flask back to Suki. "What is it?"

"Rum. It's imported and can be hard to get, unless you know the right people."

"You must know the right person."

Peals of laughter issued forth from Suki. "Doll face, I know *all* the right people."

Bethany laughed, and a smile spread across her face. Suki, her new friend, was fun.

"Come to the club with me tonight, and I'll introduce you to them." She smiled. "They'll love you."

"Tonight, I have a date. We're going to see the new Rudolph Valentino movie."

"Oh, yeah. I'm seeing it on Saturday night. Frank has some business to conduct tonight, so I'm just hanging out at the club."

"I wish I could go with you."

"Next time, doll face. You go have fun at the movie."

The phone rang, and Suki answered it.

"Hello? Oh. Hi, Frank." She winked at Bethany as she purred into the phone. "I miss you already."

Bethany decided it was time for her to go, so she gathered her old dress and slip, turned back to Suki, and whispered, "Thank you."

Suki waved at her and lay back on her bed as Bethany slipped out the door.

Back in her room, Bethany hid the ensemble

where Aunt Margaret wouldn't find it and ran herself a bubble bath. She had to get ready for her date.

Not wearing that horrible corset felt so good. She'd never wear one of those things again. To be sure she would never have to, she gathered all her other corsets and cut them to pieces while she ran the water for her bath. Then she hid them as well.

In the bath, she ran her hands down her sides and enjoyed breathing deeply the way Suki had taught her as the relaxation spread through her body.

She had a new haircut and a new dress, and tonight she'd see the movie she'd most wanted to see. Getting away from her aunt and uncle during this holiday had allowed her to meet all sorts of new friends.

Her life was getting better already, and her birthday hadn't even come yet.

Life could only get better.

"THAT DRESS IS INDECENT!" Aunt Margaret screamed at Bethany as soon as she got back from her treatment. "You'll ruin everything!"

"What's she going to ruin?" Uncle James entered the room and halted with his mouth open. Apparently Bethany's appearance had shocked him, too.

"You see, James? It's positively indecent. She is the *most* willful child. You should beat some sense into her before she ruins herself and her prospects." Her aunt paced across the room. "Today, of all days."

"What do you mean, 'today, of all days'?" Bethany crossed her arms and frowned at her aunt.

"You have your date with Mr. Rivalde tonight. Surely you haven't forgotten he invited you to see that movie. Well," Aunt Margaret huffed, placing her hands on her hips. "You're *not* going out with him wearing *that.*"

"There's nothing wrong with this dress. It's the latest fashion, and it's comfortable."

"Comfortable? Young lady, you aren't wearing a corset. Of course it's comfortable, but you aren't going out with less covering you than your nightgown. Your arms are bare, and your dress allows too much of your skin to show. It's obvious you aren't wearing a corset or a brassiere. It's indecent. Mr. Rivalde will form a different impression of you entirely. Isn't that right, James?"

Her uncle stroked his chin and contemplated Bethany. Then he stopped and met her eyes.

"Bethany, I would prefer for you to wear something more modest on your first date with Mr. Rivalde. You don't want to seem like an easy girl, I'm sure. You'll give the man the wrong impression."

"No. I don't want to seem easy, but all the girls

my age are wearing this style of dress. It doesn't mean they're easy."

"Bethany Marie, you march yourself back in there and put on your corset." He raised an eyebrow and gave her a stern look. "Your aunt will select your dress since your sense of decency has flown out the window."

I'd like to fly out of this hotel. With a weary sigh, Bethany glanced over at the open window. *I'd like to fly far away from here and go someplace where no one will care what I wear or how I do my hair. Only, I have no wings.*

"You have nothing further to say?" Aunt Margaret asked with a brisk nod. "I should hope not. Now, march along."

Bethany marched over to the wastebasket and pulled out her remaining corsets. Good thing she'd snipped and slashed all of them until there was no possible way for her to ever wear them again. The shops downstairs had already closed as well, so her aunt couldn't purchase another one for her tonight. Therefore, she wouldn't have to wear one.

Her aunt's face turned red as she stared at Bethany, and a tic spasmed beside her eye. "What have you done?"

"I've decided I'm not wearing corsets anymore," Bethany said, standing tall. "They hurt me, and I don't like them. I need room to breathe and to be able to eat."

"James, put her over your knee. We cannot allow this kind of willful disobedience."

Uncle James took one step forward and then halted, taking in Bethany's appearance again. "The girl is too old to spank, Margaret. Look at her." He cleared his throat and his face turned red. "That would be... inappropriate."

"Well," Aunt Margaret said. "If you won't, then..."

"Margaret, if she wants to go out with Richard displaying that much of herself, even after she's been warned, then let her."

"Fine."

Even though her aunt said the word, Bethany knew *everything wasn't fine. Not at all.* She would suffer repercussions later.

"At least cover yourself with a coat." Aunt Margaret stared at Bethany with disgust.

Bethany shook her head. "The weather's too warm for a coat."

"Do as your aunt says," Uncle James ordered.

ACCOMPANIED by her aunt and uncle, Bethany waited for Richard in the hotel lobby.

He widened his eyes when he saw her but didn't comment on her appearance other than to say, "You look lovely tonight, my dear."

"Thank you." She shot a glance at Aunt Margaret

and Uncle James, who stood watching them with forced smiles on their faces. The raincoat covered Bethany's arms, but she'd refused to button the coat so the golden dress peeked out from beneath it.

"I hope you don't mind walking," Richard said. "I thought the exercise would do us good. The theater isn't far."

"That's fine."

He held out his elbow, and she placed her hand in the crook of his arm. They left the hotel and headed for the theater.

"I like your hair."

"Thank you. My aunt and uncle do not approve."

"I gathered that. Rather warm for a coat, isn't it?"

"Yes, but my aunt insisted."

"I see."

He seemed to understand everything. Why couldn't her uncle be more like Richard? He really was the nicest man.

"Shall I carry it for you? If you're too warm and would like to take it off, that is."

"Why, yes. Thank you." She stopped and allowed him to ease the coat off her shoulders, and then fold it over his arm.

"Better?" He drank her in like a thirsty man as he sent her a warm smile.

"Yes, much."

They soon reached the theater. After Richard paid for the tickets, he bought Bethany some popcorn and a drink. They entered the theater, and she looked about as she waited for him to choose their seats. The place was crowded with couples, and she strained to see. Finally she spotted two empty seats down near the front. Unfortunately, Richard had already turned to a man on the end of an aisle near them and said, "Excuse us."

"Wait." Knowing sitting so far back wouldn't be nearly as good, she said, "I saw two down front."

"We'll take these. Come on."

Resigned to the fact he'd made his decision and that was that, she followed him down the row to their seats. The music had already started and the thrill of anticipation filled the air.

Bethany leaned back in her seat and held her popcorn after Richard placed her coat behind her.

"Thank you for inviting me," she said. "I've been wanting to see this movie."

"My pleasure, Bethany." He smiled. "Comfortable?"

"Yes." She smiled back at him and then reached for a bite of popcorn.

"How's your popcorn?"

"Good. Do you want some?"

"No, thank you. I don't care for any."

Bethany realized they had run out of things to say. Good thing they hadn't gone out to dinner where they'd have to talk. Once the movie started, she could relax and forget she was even on a date with him. She'd lost any interest in going on this date after meeting Paul Tollick, but she'd already agreed to this evening with Richard and backing out would have been rude and unkind. It certainly wasn't Richard's fault she wasn't interested in him in that way.

The movie started, so she pushed her thoughts aside and focused on the soaring music and sand dunes. A camp of outcasts in the desert night. Entertainers and thieves. One of the thieves threw knives at another but he didn't get hurt.

Yasmin, the daughter of Andre, head of the thieves, danced in the market to bring in money. The sheik saw her there and arranged to meet her, and she fell in love with him. He gave her a friendship ring.

When Yasmin told him he could find her in the old ruins, it reminded Bethany of meeting Paul in the park two days ago and telling him where he could see her again. She wished and hoped Paul would look for her in the park again tomorrow. It was such a surprise to bump into him after she'd had her hair cut. The way he'd touched her hair with that expression in his eyes made her feel warm inside thinking about it now.

Yasmin had to sneak away to meet her handsome boyfriend. And when Yasmin watched her new love ride off on his horse, Bethany thought of Paul walking away the first day they had met. She'd longed to call him back and to run after him. Bethany knew exactly how Yasmin was feeling about her true love.

She placed her hand against her lips. *Oh, my. Is that what I did yesterday after meeting Paul? Why, yes. I did. Am I falling in love? Is that why I keep thinking of Paul?*

In the movie, the caption read, *the son of the Sheik and Yasmin share brief, stolen meetings. Love is born.*

Bethany smiled. *How beautiful. If only Paul and I could...*

Richard placed his arm across the back of her seat and brushed the bottom of her hair.

She jumped.

"Your beautiful hair looked untouchable before." Richard lowered his voice and continued to play with her hair, the brush of his hand tickling the back of her neck and giving her goose bumps.

She shivered.

"I like it like this," he said. "It's so soft and silky."

"Thank you," she whispered, wishing he'd stop talking and leave her hair alone.

Why can't he just watch the movie? She didn't want to get in trouble for talking; she just wanted to watch the show. Besides, he'd already told her he liked her hair.

"Mmm." Richard leaned in close and breathed in the scent of her hair. "You smell good."

Goodness! What is he doing?

She wiggled away from him. He leaned back in his seat and rested his arm along the back of hers. Though he seemed to have gone back to watching the show, she believed he was also still watching her.

She tried to ignore him and focus on the movie. The popcorn now sat idle in her lap as she'd lost all taste for it. The movie soon swept her away again with the foreign and exotic romance she longed for, however, and she once more became caught up in the story.

The desert scene, with its sand dunes, swaying palm trees, and large tent with camels and horses tethered nearby mesmerized her. A man and a woman rode a horse in fast, and she decided the man must be the sheik's son. *Whoever he was, he had a commanding presence.* Men rushed up to lead his horse away, and he picked up the woman who'd ridden in with him. He carried Yasmin into the tent and tossed her onto a pile of pillows. Yasmin gasped.

Bethany gasped, too. She wished she could hear what they said to each other. *The music was so dramatic.*

Richard reached around her again and brushed her arm and the side of her breast. She inhaled sharply and froze. He dropped his hand back onto the seat.

Should she say something? What if he hadn't meant to touch her breast?

Her cheeks flushed. *How embarrassing...* for both of them if he hadn't meant to do that.

On the screen, Rudolph Valentino was even more handsome than in his movie posters. He lit a cigarette. As the scene unfolded, Yasmin tried to escape the tent but could find no way out. Bethany gasped again. The scene frightened her, but she also found it exciting. *Would the Sheik's son grab Yasmin and kiss her?*

Richard leaned close to Bethany. "You're a little spitfire beneath that sweet little girl exterior, I can tell."

He captured her lips with his. Startled, she tried to pull away, but he put his hand on the back of her neck to hold her still. She refused to open her mouth as the kiss ground on, the pressure letting her know Richard would force the intimacy whether she wanted it or not.

He slid his other hand up her leg beneath the hem of her dress, past her hose and garter belt to her bare thigh, then moved his rapidly creeping fingers even higher. Panic rose within her and she pushed her hands against his chest and broke the kiss. The popcorn spilled all over her lap and fell onto the floor.

Her chest heaving, she jumped up and said, "I'm going to the powder room."

Bethany hurried past the other couple sitting on

their row and burst out the doors into the theater lobby.

She ran out of the theater and dashed across the street without looking and hurried back to the Arlington Hotel. Several shiny new black cars with their engines running lined that side of the street.

"Hey, doll face, what's your hurry?" A man caught her arm as she stumbled on the curb, hurrying lest Mr. Rivalde catch up with her.

She looked up gasping at the tall stranger who held her arm with a firm steady grip.

Good looking in a dark, brooding way, and with a dangerous glint in his brown eyes, he put off an air of confidence and control. His shoulders were broad beneath his expensive suit. He focused his intense gaze on her, and she tottered on her heels. He tightened his grip on her arm.

"Steady now." He urged her back off the curb where she'd caught her shoe. Then he repeated, "What's the hurry?"

CHAPTER SIX

"Somebody after you?" the stranger asked. His broad shoulders filled out his dark suit. He looked down the street toward the movie theater.

"Yes! No." She darted a glance over her shoulder. Mr. Rivalde stood outside the theater, holding her coat and looking up and down the street as he searched for her. "*Yes.* I have to get away from him."

"Stick with me, kid." The man released her and opened one of the car doors. "No one will mess with you if you're with me."

He exuded strength, and Bethany had no doubt what he said he was right.

"Thank you." Filled with relief, she exhaled.

He smiled. "Get in."

She didn't know him, so she hesitated, but then

Mr. Rivalde headed down the street toward her. *He didn't look happy.*

Along the steps of the Arlington, other men in suits, some accompanied by women all dolled up for an evening out, approached their cars. Bethany didn't have time to contemplate or discuss things. The man's friends were on the move.

"Thank you." Bethany slid into the car and scooted across the seat.

The man joined her, placed his arm across the back of the seat, and surveyed the street. His arm felt more like a protective barrier or a statement rather than the beginning of a slow slide to touch her. He hadn't paid her that kind of attention.

"Doesn't look like he's still following you, doll. You gave him the slip."

Maybe so, but he knows where to find me later. She didn't say the words aloud, but the thought made her wish she never had to go back to the hotel. She had hours to kill until she had to do that. In the mean time, she would stay out as late as she could.

"Where are we going?"

"To the race track. You ever been to Oaklawn?"

"No, never."

"You're gonna love it. The horses, dinner. Mr. Capone doesn't do small time. Only the best."

"Sounds like fun."

He nodded.

The car took off, and the driver followed two

other cars. He stayed vigilant watching out the window and paid little attention to her, though he kept his arm across the back of the seat.

How odd that he hadn't even asked her name. Perhaps he wasn't interested in her. Well, she could be bold, instead of shy, and ask the question herself.

"I'm Bethany Robinson. What's your name?"

"Rocco."

Was that his first name or his last name? She'd never heard that name before, but she wasn't about to ask about it. Rocco wasn't in a conversational mood. He was too intent on whatever he was looking at out the windows.

She reached into her bag for the red lipstick, pulled off the lid, and leaned forward so she could see herself in the car's rearview mirror. She'd known better than to apply the lipstick at the hotel where her aunt might have taken it away.

The driver watched her in the mirror. Blushing, she glanced away and finished applying it, then sat back in her seat to look out the window.

They soon arrived at the Oaklawn Race Track. Once the driver parked the car, Rocco said, "Wait here until I tell you to get out."

One man stepped out of each car, scanned the area, and then spoke to the people inside.

Rocco turned to the people inside their car and said, "All clear."

The others started to get out, and he reached in a

hand to help Bethany onto the curb. He gazed into her eyes. "Come on, Bethany."

So he had been paying attention. She placed her hand in his and enjoyed the way he helped her out of the car. He shut the door with one fluid movement and ushered her ahead of him with just his fingertips on her back.

His touch didn't feel creepy. No, more like a man taking control and taking care of her in a matter of fact way without wanting anything from her. *It felt nice.* She could see why Suki found these men so attractive. They dressed sharply, they had elegant manners, and they were protective of their women. She didn't feel like a commodity, something to be owned. She was here because she wanted to be, no pressure.

"Who's the dame?" a man asked Rocco.

He reached for her with one hand, placed it on her back, and urged her forward. "Mr. Capone, this is Bethany Robinson."

"She's too young." A frown crossed Mr. Capone's face.

Oh, no. They'll send me away. Bethany met his eyes. "I'll be eighteen on Sunday."

"Make sure you know what you're doing." Mr. Capone shook his head as if shaking off something he didn't want to look at, then pinned Rocco with a piercing glance. "No foul ups."

"Yes, sir." Rocco nodded. "I have it under control."

"You'd better." Mr. Capone walked away, and everyone else followed in his wake.

Wait. Mr. Capone. Was he the man Paul had warned her about? *The man Paul had said was so dangerous? He must be.* Bethany could sense it now. The element of danger. She sensed it on all of them. Every one of these men was dangerous, but that danger wasn't directed at her. If anything, she was safe here in their presence. And even though she was young, Mr. Capone had just accepted her into his circle. Rocco seemed pleased, and everything was under control.

He guided her along, silent and strong, just as he had before. She'd like to see Richard Rivalde try to put his hands all over her now. *Rocco would never allow that.* He'd made it clear simply by his presence that she was under his protection.

She finally felt safe again.

PAUL COULDN'T BELIEVE his eyes. He'd gone to the racetrack to wait for the gang members and watched them as usual with little emotion, the detached observation of a detective, when Bethany Robinson stepped out of one of the cars holding on to Rocco's hand.

Then Bethany, the sweet little blonde with the beautiful blue eyes, turned all of that sweetness toward Rocco. Wanting to smash something, Paul curled his hands into fists.

What the hell is she doing here? With Rocco? What the hell is she thinking?

She appeared to be here by choice and was apparently having a good time, even though she'd directed that sweet, innocent smile at a dirty criminal who could gun down a man at any second without blinking an eye. The idea made Paul sick to his stomach.

Bethany had no idea what she'd gotten herself mixed up in. What the hell was Rocco doing with her anyway? Innocent young girls weren't his style, although he did like them blonde and pretty. He also liked to have them frequently. Rocco was a man of large appetites. He not only liked to have women frequently, he also liked to have his blondes more than one at a time.

Innocent Bethany was in way over her head.

The question was, what was Paul going to do about it? He couldn't blow his cover, so for now; he had to resign himself to watching them.

They reached a private area of the racetrack and knowing Bethany was inside where he could no longer see her turned his guts. He couldn't see what Rocco was doing to her.

He needed a cigarette, and he didn't have one. He'd given up the habit over a year ago.

WHILE BETHANY WATCHED THE RACES, Rocco explained how they worked and how to place a bet. Though he didn't invite her to place one. He bet big money and won, too. The men all knew the names of the horses and the jockeys, and all of them placed bets. They betted quietly, and Bethany got the impression all of the bets involved big money.

They enjoyed juicy steaks, baked potatoes, and salads, and the waiters served everyone cocktails. Bethany had no idea what to order to drink.

Rocco said, "Bring her a gin fizz, and I'll take a rye whiskey."

Her gin fizz turned out to be a sweet, fizzy drink with a kick. Bethany sipped it as she ate, and by the time she was full, she'd finished the drink and felt warm and relaxed, with a tendency to giggle.

Rocco smiled at her every time she did, and the corners of his eyes crinkled up.

"The horses are so beautiful. Wish I had a horse," Bethany said.

Rocco winked at her. "Stick with me, doll, and I just might buy you one."

"I have a birthday coming up soon. This week."

"And you'll be eighteen. I know. You already told me."

"Oh, I did?"

"Yes, you did. Aren't you going to finish your steak? You didn't eat much."

"Oh, I'm full. I never eat much. My aunt doesn't allow it." She hiccupped.

The waitress came over with a steaming cup of java and placed it in front of Bethany.

"Coffee? I don't drink coffee."

Rocco looked at Mr. Capone, who nodded at him.

"Tonight, doll, you're going to learn. That drink went to your head a little too fast."

"Oh, I don't think I want it. I really am full."

"Mr. Capone sent it to you. Just sip it." He pushed a bowl and small pitcher toward her. "Here's some cream and sugar. Try adding a little of each until it tastes good to you."

Obviously bemused, he smiled as she dropped sugar cube after sugar cube into her coffee, stirred it, then took a sip and tried again.

When she finally managed to drink half of it, Rocco pushed his chair back and stood. The others all did the same. "Time to go. Have you ever been to The Southern Club?"

"No. Are we going there now? Is there dancing?"

"Yes. You like to dance?"

"Suki promised to teach me."

"You know Suki?"

"Yes."

"You're going to fit right in." He slipped his arm around her and moved toward the door.

They all got back into their shiny black cars and headed to The Southern Club. Just as they had last time, everyone moved in the same routine, with a few men getting out of the cars, looking about, and then giving the others the go ahead.

Rocco opened the door and reached in for Bethany. She placed her hand in his and stepped out. Ever vigilant, he didn't stop surveying their surroundings even as he placed his hand on the small of her back and guided her into the club.

Music poured out of the place as flappers and their dates made their way inside. All the ladies wore pretty summer dresses with dropped waists and beads and long ropes of pearls.

Inside the club, white tablecloths covered the round tables and crystal candleholders holding lit candles sat in the middle of each one. Everyone had some form of drink, and the crystal glasses and wine goblets caught the light of the flickering candles.

Large chandeliers lit up the dance floor in front of the band. The musicians played the Charleston as dancers stepped high. Bethany couldn't wait to learn that dance.

Rocco led her to a table near the front of the dance floor marked by a *reserved* sign. One of the waiters plucked the sign off the table and then held out a chair for her.

Suki came over to her. "Bethany, you're here. I see you've met Rocco. That's Frank."

The man Suki pointed out, who must have been Frank, walked over to whisper in Mr. Capone's ear. Mr. Capone nodded, and Frank went over to the bar to talk to the bartender.

"They've got some business to discuss," Suki said. "Do you want some champagne?"

"None for her tonight, Suki," Rocco said. "She was spiffilcated before we even left the track. Can't send my little baby home in that condition so soon."

"Yours, Rocco?"

"Mine."

"Want her all to yourself, do you?"

"As I said, *mine.*"

"That was fast. Over the Canton twins so soon?"

"Leave it, Suki."

"Come on, doll face," Suki turned to Bethany, who was bewildered by their whole conversation. "You ready to dance?"

"Oh, yes." Bethany had been tapping her toes. "I can't wait to learn the Charleston."

"That's not even the newest dance." Suki sipped her champagne, and then set her glass on the table. "It's the Black Bottom. Come on. I'll teach you."

Bethany enjoyed learning all the new dances while Rocco watched from his table. A few minutes passed, and then someone tapped her on the shoulder. She turned to see who it was.

A policeman.

She stopped dancing and froze on the dance floor. The dancers around her moved away as if she had the plague. *Oh, this isn't good. I'm in big trouble.*

"Miss Robinson, this isn't the place for a woman your age." He gestured at the tables where Mr. Capone and his men sat. Mr. Capone leaned toward Rocco and said something as they both watched her with the policeman. "Have you been keeping company with those men?"

Rocco who'd been half out of his seat, leaned back, restrained by whatever Mr. Capone said to him.

"No, daddy, she's with me." Suki interrupted the policeman and threaded her arm through Bethany's and winked at him. "She just wants to learn the new dances. See?"

"That's right," Bethany said. "Suki promised to teach me the dances."

"So she's been a good little doll this evening," Suki said. "In a couple of days, she'll be eighteen, and then she can do whatever she wants."

"Be that as it may, she's not eighteen yet. I'm sure Mr. Capone doesn't want to have to deal with this kind of situation while he's on vacation trying to relax." He nodded at Suki and then addressed Bethany again. "Your aunt and uncle are worried. They filed a missing persons report. You'll have to come with me."

"Yes, sir." Cheeks blazing, Bethany walked toward the door with the policeman. Rocco's steady gaze stayed upon her as she turned toward Suki and mouthed, "Thank you."

Suki blew her a kiss and winked.

CHAPTER SEVEN

The policeman walked Bethany back to the Arlington Hotel where her aunt and uncle waited. With every step, she dreaded the confrontation to come a little more.

She hated that she'd worried them and hoped Aunt Margaret didn't have another one of her terrible headaches. Making them sick with worry hadn't been her intention. She'd just wanted to get away from Mr. Rivalde. If he hadn't put his hands all over her and scared her, she would've been back at the hotel by now reading her book. She did owe them an apology.

Once she and the policeman reached the hotel, they rode the elevator up to the fifth floor. The policeman knocked on the door of her aunt and uncle's hotel room.

His expression stony, Uncle James opened the door.

"Here she is, safe and sound," the policeman said.

"Thank you, officer." Uncle James stood aside to allow Bethany to walk into the room.

The police officer bobbed his head and turned to leave. "Good evening, then."

Aunt Margaret's face was white with rage. The minute Uncle James closed the door, she rounded on Bethany. "How dare you?"

"Leaving Mr. Rivalde in the theater was inexcusable." Uncle James tone was severe. "You embarrassed him, embarrassed me, and embarrassed your aunt."

Bethany's coat lay across the bed, but she saw no sign of Mr. Rivalde.

"We raised you to have better manners," Aunt Margaret said.

"I'm extremely disappointed in you." Uncle James said. "You will apologize to Richard."

"I had to leave. He was..." She wrapped her arms around herself and forced out the words. "He was... *touching* me."

"Liar." Aunt Margaret backhanded her across the face.

Shocked and stung, Bethany froze, her eyes wide and her shoulders shaking. Though her parents had spanked her many times as a child, no one had ever hit her in the face before.

Uncle James appeared shocked, too, but recovered quickly and said, "You're not in a position to accuse a man I've known for years of such a thing. Not when you run with known criminals and carry on, drinking and running wild. *You're* the one who's out of control."

"But he--"

"Not another word out of you." Uncle James raised his hand.

Tears filled her eyes.

"You will apologize to Mr. Rivalde," Aunt Margaret said.

Her arms dropped and she blinked the tears away. "I will not."

"You will apologize," Uncle James said. "And you will accept his offer of marriage."

"Marriage?" Bethany squeaked, barely getting the word out.

"Yes, marriage. Richard is willing to forgive you and forget this evening's escapade, and he's offered to save your reputation by giving you his good name."

"I don't have a reputation. You never let me leave the house. No one even knows me."

"Don't be ridiculous." Aunt Margaret said. "You ruined your reputation the minute you cut your hair and started running around this town half dressed."

"You think I should *marry* that man? I just met him. He had his hands all over me at that theater. I couldn't bear to spend another evening alone with him, let alone marry him." She turned toward her uncle. "Just because you have a business deal with him doesn't... oh."

She stepped back and put her hands over her mouth to cover her gasp.

"She's out of control, James," Aunt Margaret said.

"You've been pushing me toward him." Bethany pointed at her aunt, and then turned to face her uncle. Eyes wide, she stood shaking as the truth grew within her. "Your business deal involves *me*. It's about my inheritance."

"Don't be silly." Her aunt stood. "You're too high strung tonight, and your thoughts are out of control." She moved toward the door and addressed Uncle James. "There's no point trying to reason with her when she's like this."

"We'll be back when you've had time to calm down and become more reasonable." Uncle James said.

"You mean when I calm down and agree to do what you want."

"I suggest you get some sleep," Uncle James said. "It's past your bedtime."

"I am *not* a child."

"You're behaving like a willful child." Aunt Margaret gathered her purse. "You will stay in this room until you come to your senses." She turned to Uncle James. "James. The phone."

Uncle James pulled the phone out of the wall, and Aunt Margaret picked up Bethany's purse. Then they left the room and locked her in from the outside.

"No!" She ran to the door and twisted the handle, but it wouldn't open. She banged on the door. "You can't lock me in here."

She didn't have a key. They'd caged her here in her own hotel room. Hot tears rolled down her cheeks. She flung herself on the bed. *It's so unfair. It's all so unfair.*

She burst into tears and cried herself to sleep.

THE CHIRPING of birds and the sun pouring through the window woke Bethany. No one had closed the drapes last night. She'd fallen asleep fully dressed. Her eyes were puffy and tired, and the tracks of her tears streaked her face. Her head and stomach hurt. She needed something to eat. *A piece of toast, anything.*

She waited, but no one came. No one brought her any food or anything to drink. *Her aunt and uncle must have told the staff to stay away.*

Her stomach sloshed from all the water she drank after she awakened. At least she had a water glass and a sink so she wouldn't dry up from the heat in the room. The day was so hot. She peeled off her clothing from the night before and pulled on her coolest, thinnest cotton nightgown, then washed everything else out in the sink and hung it up to dry.

She was both hungry and slightly nauseated. Her headache had gone away after drinking plenty of water and taking an aspirin powder. Oh, if she could only have a roll or even just some crackers. *Anything.*

She hated being locked inside this room. How long could this go on? If she were at home, they could lock her in her room for a very long time, but here, if they kept her locked up too long, surely that would draw attention. Besides, tomorrow was her birthday, and she'd turn eighteen. They couldn't do what they wanted to her once she was of age, could they?

Through the open window, the song *Bye, Bye Blackbird* drifted in along with the summer heat. Bethany sang along with Gene Autry, "Blackbird, blackbird, singing the blues all day…"

She went over to the window and leaned on the windowsill, listening and enjoying what little breeze caressed her heated skin.

"Pack up all my cares and woes, here I go… " Her toes tapped as they always did when a song spoke to her as her voice carried out the window. "No one here can love and understand me…"

The song expressed so much of what she felt. If

only someone would hear her and come let her out of this blasted room.

Yet no one came.

The day finally passed, and dinnertime arrived. Her stomach hurt just like it had when she was small and Aunt Margaret punished her by sending her to bed without supper. Back then; another whole day might pass until they allowed her to eat again. At that point, she'd agree to whatever her aunt wanted. They'd finally allow her to join them at supper the next night, and her aunt would imply that Bethany had eaten earlier that day when she hadn't. Uncle James always believed her aunt over her.

This time, however, Uncle James had helped Aunt Margaret lock her in. So now she knew his failure to protect her from her aunt in the past hadn't been because he'd been unaware of what Aunt Margaret had done. *No, he'd either agreed with her aunt or he just didn't care enough to intervene.*

Bethany would *never* agree to what they wanted this time, no matter what they did to her. She'd starve to death first. *I'm not the one who is out of control and unreasonable. They are.*

Something deep within her soul told her that treating a child this way was wrong. Though she was no longer a child, she remembered so many instances like this; times when they'd starved her. *It was wrong. So very wrong.* She'd done nothing to deserve it.

Parents or guardians should feed children until they are no longer hungry. They should never call their children names. Or slap them in the face.

When she had children of her own, she'd never treat them that way. She'd love them with everything she had.

Also, Mr. Rivalde should not have put his hands on her that way. It had made her feel dirty and used. Dear God, if that was how he behaved on a first date, how much worse would he act if she married him? She had to get away.

Neither her aunt nor her uncle had believed her, and neither one of them had asked how she was or expressed any relief that she was okay. For a family supposedly *so* worried about her, the only emotion Aunt Margaret and Uncle James had displayed when she'd arrived back at the room safe and sound was anger.

Bethany decided to remain quiet until tomorrow, when she turned eighteen. Then she'd fly far, far away. She'd find an attorney and ask him to contact Uncle James about her inheritance.

Right now she had no money, but she would find a job. Maybe one of her new friends would help her. *Suki knew everybody.* If only Bethany had a way to get a message to Suki. *She'd find a way to get me out of this room.*

Standing at the window on the fifth floor looking down, Bethany could find no way out, no way to get a message to anyone. *What about Paul?* Had he gone to the park today and waited for her, then wondered why she didn't show? Or had he forgotten all about her?

She wished she could talk to Paul. He wouldn't let her aunt and uncle keep her locked up like this with no food to eat, but she couldn't call him or Suki or anyone else, since her uncle had taken the phone.

All she could do was wait. She opened her book to read again about exotic places and imagine she was anywhere but here. Reading would make time pass faster and help her forget she was hungry, at least for a while.

The sun went down, and still no one came. When the dinner hour passed without anyone bringing her anything to eat, Bethany ran a cool bath and prepared for bed.

No one would come tonight.

She bathed and washed her hair and vowed to get a good night's sleep so she'd be rested for her birthday the next day.

THE NEXT MORNING, someone turned a key in the lock and opened the door.

Aunt Margaret stood in the doorway looking in, her lips pursed.

Bethany sat on the bed, wearing her new golden

dress, her book open on her lap.

"Well, I'm glad to see you've settled down."

She didn't reply. She simply looked at her aunt.

"Do you have anything to say for yourself?"

Bethany gave her aunt a bland look, kept her thoughts to herself, and tried not to be as readable as usual. Then she shrugged.

"I promised we'd shop for a birthday dress," Aunt Margaret said. "Since you insist you will no longer wear corsets, you must find some other sort of suitable support."

Bethany closed the book and stood. Her aunt peered at her as if trying to read her mood and thoughts, but Bethany gave nothing away.

"Well, come along then."

Bethany walked toward the door, and her stomach gave a loud growl.

Her aunt smirked. "I suppose you'd like to have a small breakfast before we go."

Without speaking, Bethany turned away.

Just outside the door, her aunt halted. "Well, do you want breakfast, or don't you?"

"Yes, ma'am."

"I won't have you being sullen all day and refusing to speak to anyone."

"Yes, ma'am." Bethany followed her aunt, but kept repeating one word over and over inside her head as soon as she walked out the door.

Free. Free. Free.

CHAPTER EIGHT

Bethany vowed her aunt and uncle would never lock her in again. They couldn't lock her into a room she refused to enter. She'd never let them starve her again, either. She kept these thoughts to herself like a secret treasure she'd never share. Bethany couldn't keep down the sense of elation bubbling up within her. Today was her eighteenth birthday.

Never again would she have to do everything her aunt and uncle wanted her to do. She would wear what she wanted to wear, cut her hair, and go out with any man she chose to date.

The world was wide open. Anything was possible.

However much her parents had left her, she knew it would be enough to buy new dresses, shoes, and hats. She'd look like other girls her age. Why, she might even go on to college. Or get married, if she met the right man.

The important thing was that from this day forward, she'd make her own decisions.

Once a waiter seated Bethany and her aunt in the dining room downstairs, Aunt Margaret waved away the menus.

"We will both have grapefruit, toast, and tea."

"No grapefruit for me," Bethany said. "I'll have a poached egg on toast."

"We also have Eggs Benedict," the waiter said.

She smiled. "You do? Well, that sounds lovely. I'll have that, with hot cocoa. And do you have whipped cream?"

"Yes, we do."

"Excellent. Today is my birthday, so I'd like whipped cream on my hot cocoa."

"Of course." The waiter smiled. "Happy birthday, miss."

"Thank you." Bethany beamed at him. "I'm eighteen today."

"A very special birthday indeed." He bowed and went off to put in their orders.

Her aunt had narrowed eyes while Bethany ordered but didn't comment until after the waiter left. "Eggs Benedict is terribly fattening. The Hollandaise sauce alone... and whipped cream, too?"

"Yes. A perfect birthday breakfast."

"Humph." Her aunt sat back in her chair as the waiter placed her napkin in her lap. "Your uncle is in a meeting this morning, but we will see him at dinner. We've invited Richard to join us to celebrate your birthday. I hope you're prepared to apologize to him."

"I will apologize to him when he apologizes to me."

Her aunt's jaw dropped open. Then she snapped it shut.

The waiter brought their tea and hot cocoa, and they sat in silence. That ordinarily would have felt oppressive to Bethany, but not today. Today, she wouldn't let anything ruin her birthday. She simply wouldn't allow it.

Bethany didn't count her bites this time. She'd never allow anyone to control her portion sizes again. How many bites she took or how much she did or did not eat didn't matter. For once, she would enjoy her food. She ate with gusto, and her aunt's frown continued to grow.

Soon, her aunt's face was as sour as the grapefruit she'd tried to order for Bethany. The fruit suited her aunt and was Bethany's least favorite breakfast food.

"Well, you certainly gobbled down your breakfast like a greedy little girl," Aunt Margaret said.

"It was good, and I was hungry."

"That should hold you until dinner then." Her

aunt pushed away from the table and stood. "Come along. We have much to do before this evening."

Bethany wiped her mouth with her napkin, laid it on the table, and followed her aunt.

AT THE DRESS SHOP, her aunt approached the shopkeeper. "We have a dilemma. My niece has decided her corsets and dresses no longer suit her, but she cannot be running about town without a brassiere."

"All the other girls do," Bethany said.

The shopkeeper took in Bethany's appearance and said, "Perhaps a compromise between the two extremes is in order."

Aunt Margaret pursed her lips and nodded.

What a surprise. Bethany had never known her aunt to compromise on anything. She bobbed her head in agreement.

"First, we must measure you for a brassiere," the shopkeeper said. "Many of the ladies find the Maidenform brasseries to be much more comfortable than a corset. We also have the Boyishform brasserie if you prefer the flatter look the younger girls are wearing. After we fit you, I'll show you our dresses."

"All right. I've been wrapping gauze around--"

"Oh, dear," the woman interrupted, shaking her head. "That doesn't give you enough support."

"I told her it was positively indecent. A lady *must*

wear undergarments." Aunt Margaret's voice became shriller with each word.

"Yes, well... you've made an excellent decision to come here today. You have come to the right place." The shopkeeper's calm, reassuring tone soothed Bethany. "You see, my dear, the flat chested look so many of the young ladies wear today can be accomplished without resorting to gauze. Breasts must be supported and protected for good health and for comfort. Especially since the newer dances are so vigorous."

Bethany had to admit that getting used to going bare breasted beneath her dress had been difficult, even with gauze wrapped around her to bind them. The gauze had moved when she danced and wasn't all that comfortable. Although anything was better than a corset, a garment she'd grown to detest.

By the time she and Aunt Margaret finished shopping, Bethany had two new brassieres that fit, one in the regular style so she could still wear her older dresses, and one in the flattened style with thinner straps to wear under her new dresses, along with a new slip, and a pale blue dress with short sleeves, a dropped waist, and a hem that ended just below her knee. The dress was soft and comfortable. Both the shopkeeper and her aunt said it looked good on Bethany. Looking in the mirror and turning from side to side to make the skirt swirl, she agreed.

Her aunt paid for the purchases.

As they left the shop, she said, "Since you've decided not to wear any more corsets, I expect you to wear a bra at all times. No more running about half naked."

Bethany nearly retorted that what she did or did not wear was no longer up to her aunt, but she wisely held back her reply. Her aunt had just bought her multiple birthday presents and even compromised about the brasseries, and she didn't want to seem ungrateful. So she simply said, "Thank you for the birthday gifts."

"You're welcome," her aunt said.

The lunch hour had passed and Bethany was hungry, but she knew better than to mention food to her aunt. Instead, she accompanied Aunt Margaret back to the hotel.

Once they arrived, Bethany hurried over to the front desk.

"The phone is out in my room," she said. "I need you to repair it, please."

Her aunt came up behind Bethany. She didn't say anything but fixed her cold gaze upon Bethany's back.

"We'll send maintenance up right away, miss," the clerk said. "Is there anything else?"

"Yes, please send up the lunch special, whatever that is today."

"That would be cream of salmon soup, cabbage salad sandwiches, gingerbread, and tea."

"It sounds lovely. Yes, please do send that up."

"Of course, miss."

Bethany turned to face her aunt.

"And just how are you paying for that?" Aunt Margaret asked. "Will you put it on the room so your uncle can pay for it? You know we don't order room service."

"He can take it out of my inheritance if he needs to."

"Don't be ridiculous."

"I'm not being ridiculous at all. I'm going to have lunch in my room while they fix the phone, and then I am going to take a nice long bath and get ready for dinner. I'll wear the blue dress tonight. It's such a pretty one." Wanting to smooth the prickliness away, she gave her aunt a smile.

"Humph." Her aunt retreated into silence. *Who knew what she was thinking?*

Being an independent woman didn't have to include being unkind, even to her aunt, but Bethany *would* eat lunch and have a phone reinstalled in her room.

Repairing the phone took much longer than she'd expected. The workman still hadn't installed it when the time came for her to take her bath and get ready for dinner. He said the damage was worse than they'd expected, and that he'd return tomorrow and finish the job.

Bethany took her bath, thinking of how she'd

never allow anyone to lock her inside her room again. She had to get the key from her aunt, and she didn't want to be without a phone. She just had to get through the evening, get the key, and tomorrow she'd have a phone again. She would not be cut off from her new friends or anyone else.

Bathed, powdered, and primped, she met her aunt and uncle in the hallway and headed downstairs with them. Mr. Rivalde met them in the lobby. He looked at Bethany as if nothing untoward had ever occurred between them.

Well he might fool her aunt and uncle, but he wasn't fooling her for a minute. She would be civil to him, but she didn't trust him one bit.

"Happy Birthday, Bethany," he said.

"Thank you."

The headwaiter led them to their table, and they all sat down.

The pianist in the corner played a variety of music. Dinner was a quiet affair, with everyone talking about books, music, and art. Mr. Rivalde was knowledgeable about all three. Everyone was on their best social behavior, overly polite to one another, as if walking on eggshells. She supposed they all were.

Then their waiter brought out a cake covered with lit candles, and he and the rest of the wait staff assembled to sing *Happy Birthday* to Bethany. The pianist accompanied them.

The whole room applauded when they were done. She blew out the candles and made a special secret wish. The waiter sliced and served the delicious cake.

After Bethany finished eating her slice, Mr. Rivalde turned to her. "I have a birthday gift for you. Though this is much more than a birthday present."

He handed her a small present. She took it with a sinking feeling in the pit of her stomach.

I hope it isn't what I think it is. She tore open the wrapping paper and opened the small box. Her stomach dropped like a stone. He'd given her an engagement ring. A very large diamond surrounded by smaller stones.

"Will you marry me?"

"No." She shook her head and held the gift out to him. "I cannot accept this. I cannot marry you."

When he didn't take the ring, she set it on the table in front of him. She didn't care if he took it or not. She didn't want it.

"Bethany, you must reconsider," Uncle James said. "Mr. Rivalde is a steady, responsible man who will care well for you and your family interests."

Aunt Margaret pursed her lips. Her frown deepened.

"Yes, Uncle James, about my family interests, such as my inheritance... you certainly cannot expect me to make any decision affecting something I know so little about."

"It is best to let the men who understand such things handle them," her aunt said. "Your uncle has handled your interests well all these years. You should trust him."

"I do trust him."

"Thank you for that," her uncle said.

"You've always been honest with me in the past," Bethany said. "And I expect you to tell me about exactly what we're talking about."

"What do you want to know?"

"I want to know the amount of my inheritance, where it is, and what my rights are now that I'm of age."

"That's reasonable, but we should discuss such matters in a more private setting. Not here."

"Tomorrow, then."

"Tomorrow, I have meetings. We should wait until after we return home. I'll set up a meeting with our attorney to go over the terms of your father's will."

"Fine. But won't you tell me something of what we're talking about before then? Give me an idea?"

"Your uncle is on vacation, Bethany," Aunt Margaret said, "and you've given him more stress already than he should've had to deal with while we're here in Hot Springs."

"So neither of you is willing to tell me anything." Bethany frowned.

"This isn't the time," her uncle said.

They were dancing around her, putting it off. Treating her like a child, the way they always had. She grew angry.

"Have you told *him?*" Bethany jerked her thumb angrily at Mr. Rivalde. "I'm sure you have, since you're all so ready for me to marry him. I'm willing to bet it's part of your merger."

"Don't be rude." Her uncle pinned her with a thunderous look.

"My inheritance has nothing to do with him. It's *my* money. I'm not marrying anyone or agreeing to anything until I know exactly what is involved."

Mr. Rivalde stood. "I didn't intend to ruin your birthday dinner with my presence, but I can see that you are agitated. I bid you another happy birthday and good evening."

"Bethany Marie," her aunt said with a gasp. "Apologize to Mr. Rivalde at once."

She ignored her aunt. "Thank you for the birthday wishes. Good evening."

Mr. Rivalde walked away, leaving Bethany alone with her aunt and uncle, who both wore stony faces.

"If you're quite done," her aunt said. "That's enough for one evening."

"Yes, I'm done," Bethany stood. "Thank you for the birthday dinner and the gifts."

"You're welcome," her uncle said.

They left the restaurant and headed up to their rooms, riding the elevator in silence as Bethany ignored their stony expressions. On the fifth floor, outside her door, Bethany held out her hand for the key to her room.

Aunt Margaret smirked and refused to hand it over.

"Really?" Bethany shook her head. "And you tell me *I'm* childish." She shrugged. "Well, I'm not tired, so I'll go down to the lobby bar to people watch for a while."

"You cannot sit in the bar unescorted."

"I certainly can. Women do it all the time."

"James, do something."

"I will escort you."

"Fine. Then we can discuss my inheritance."

By the look on his face, she knew she had him. If he went with her, she'd badger him about it, and he knew it. Letting her go on her own was one way to avoid that.

"I'm tired." He turned away and headed for his door. "Margaret, Bethany is of age and can go where she wishes."

"Selfish, ungrateful girl."

Bethany didn't wait any longer. If her aunt wouldn't give her the key to her own room, then fine. She didn't have to stay here and chance getting locked in again. She ran to the elevator and punched the button. When the door opened, she stepped in and rode down to the lobby. Tonight was Sunday, so nothing was going on. No band, no dancing, just people sitting in the bar enjoying their drinks and chatting.

At the bar, she ordered a soda and sat at an empty table. She'd sipped about a third of her drink when Rocco slid into the seat across from her.

"There's the birthday princess."

She turned her face up toward him and beamed a smile.

"Where've you been? I've been looking for you."

"You have?"

He nodded as he took her in. "You're not an easy dame to find."

"My aunt and uncle locked me in my room after that policeman brought me back and didn't let me out until today."

"I'd have sprung you if I'd known. You should've called me or Suki."

"How could I with no phone? My uncle ripped it out of the wall when they locked me up. The hotel is supposed to fix the phone, but they hadn't finished repairing it when we went to dinner."

"That won't happen again. I'll look out for you, doll."

"Thank you." Tears filled her eyes. "I've never had anyone look out for me and protect me like you do."

"No more tears." He reached for her hand. "No more fear."

Blinking away her tears, she nodded and smiled. "No more."

"Birthday girls should always smile and be happy."

She broadened her smile.

He reached into his pocket. "I was looking for you so I could give you your birthday present."

"You got me a present?"

He pulled out a flat black velvet box with a white silk bow tied around it and handed it to her, watching her eyes.

"Oh, my goodness." Bethany widened her eyes and reached for it. She hurried to untie the ribbon, knowing it must be something special to be wrapped so fine. Opening the lid, she gasped.

A long strand of white pearls lay inside.

"I noticed you weren't wearing any jewelry the other night. All the other girls have pearls."

"Oh, they're beautiful." Amazed, she looked up at him. He was so nice and generous. "I love them."

"Put them on." His eyes hooded. "I want to see them on you."

"Oh, yes." She reached inside the box and took them out. "Thank you."

She placed them around her neck and let them hang down the front of her dress. The weight of the pearls felt nice against her blue dress and looked lovely, too. They rested in between her breasts and hung all the way to her belly button. Another way to wear them might have been to knot them, as some of the girls did, but they looked so pretty this way.

She'd never had pearls before. She only had little girl sized rings and a necklace that no longer fit. Aunt Margaret had yet to hand over any jewelry that had belonged to Bethany's mother.

Rocco swept his gaze from her face all the way down to the end of the necklace and back up again. She could tell by his expression that he enjoyed what he saw.

Paul watched Bethany all evening.

He first wondered about the man who joined her and her aunt and uncle for dinner and then proposed. *She'd said nothing about having a suitor.* When she turned down the ring, however, Paul's heart rose in his chest. *She wasn't going to marry the man. Her aunt and uncle had apparently promoted the match, but she would have none of it.*

He was proud of her for standing up to them.

He fingered the present in his pocket. Yesterday, he'd found the delicate pair of butterfly earrings the color of her eyes, and they'd reminded him of her and the day they'd met amid the butterflies. He'd known he had to buy them for her, for her birthday, and he'd hoped she would not only like them but would remember that day as fondly as he did. They'd seemed like the perfect gift for her.

Bethany went back upstairs with her aunt and uncle before he had a chance to talk with her, so he found a spot in the lobby to wait in case she came back down.

He didn't have to wait long.

She reappeared after only a few minutes and settled in at a table in the bar.

He got up and moved toward her, hoping to surprise her, but halted when Rocco entered the bar and headed straight for her. He seated himself across from her, and Paul edged back into the shadows.

When she told Rocco her aunt and uncle had locked her inside her hotel room like a caged bird, Paul's gut clenched.

She'd told him the truth in the park and then denied it. He'd bet money that wasn't the first time they'd locked her up either, despite what she'd said.

He wished he'd known they'd locked her in that hotel room yesterday. He would've helped her get free. Then she wouldn't be sitting in this bar now with Rocco, her sweet innocent face turned toward his, gratitude brimming in her beautiful blue eyes.

When she accepted the pearls, his heart sank. Surely she'd hand them back to him the same way she'd handed the ring back to the other man at dinner. She didn't. Instead, she put them on and smiled with joy.

What the hell was she thinking? Did she know what she'd just done? Did she want to be a gangster's moll? Whether she'd realized what she was doing or not, she'd crossed a line of no return. Rocco would claim her now.

Every man on the planet was trying to give her jewelry tonight. She was beautiful. In fact, she was a real prize, and that was obvious to the rich and powerful men drawn to her.

He fingered the butterfly earrings in his pocket. They seemed small and inexpensive compared to what the other two men could give her. *She'd been born to money and maybe that was what she wanted.* He could never give her that on a detective's salary.

Rocco pulled Bethany's hand up to his mouth to kiss it, and Paul told himself he should walk away, right now.

Yet he couldn't. Not until he knew she was safe.

CHAPTER NINE

Rocco took Bethany's hand. "I've always wanted a gal like you."

"You have?"

"Sure, doll. You're the cat's pajamas."

Bethany blushed.

"Stick with me, doll face. I'll love you and treat you like a queen."

He brought her hand up to his lips and kissed it. She sighed at the romantic gesture and the tickle across her skin. He lowered her hand, never letting go of it, and watched her from across the table.

"Rocco?"

"Yes, doll?" He rubbed his thumb across the back of her hand. It was a pleasant sensation, a distracting one, but she pressed on.

"Your job. A friend told me it's really dangerous. Have you ever thought of doing something else?"

"Baby, this is what I do." He tightened his hold on her hand, then winked at her and grinned. "You're a sweetheart for worrying about me. Don't you worry your pretty little head. I always take care of things. I'll bring home the dough, and plenty of it. You don't need to worry about a thing. I'll take care of you."

He pulled her hand toward his lips again. This was all happening so fast. Bethany wasn't sure what to say or do. She'd been out with Rocco once, and meeting up with him tonight had been a complete surprise. This was all so unexpected.

The bartender stopped by their table and whispered something in Rocco's ear.

Rocco released her hand, listened, nodded, and then turned back to her. "I have something to take care of, and I'm not sure how long it'll take."

"Oh. Yes, your job." Bethany had no idea what he did exactly, and he didn't talk or behave as if he'd ever tell her. She bit back the curiosity that filled her.

"Some jobs come up suddenly. You'll get used to it." He stood and pushed his chair under the table. "Much as I'd love to end your birthday a different way, I have to go now."

"I understand." She stood, too. "Thank you for the birthday gift."

"How about a quick kiss before I go?" He'd moved around the table, reached for her, and pulled her close.

His lips descended on hers. Strong, passionate lips that tasted of mint. Within his arms she felt small, as if the strength of his arms and his chest might crush her at any minute. He held her firmly and securely as his tongue sought entry between her lips.

She gave way to his masculine forceful persuasion and parted her lips. His tongue moved inside her mouth, tasting, touching. Then all at once she felt as if he were taking her air, and a panic rose in her chest.

He pulled back suddenly and said, "Wish we had time for more."

She gasped and drew in a lungful of air, her heart racing and her eyes wide as she gaped up at him without speaking.

"I have to go." He cupped her chin in his large hand. "You shouldn't stay in this bar by yourself."

He was right. Men around them had their eyes on her, especially now after he'd kissed her. She hadn't noticed any of them watching her before.

"I'll go up to my room."

"Good girl." He pulled out a wad of money and tossed a bill onto the table, and then waited until she picked up her clutch purse and the box her necklace had come in. Then he looked up at the clock and said, "I have to run, doll. I'll call you tomorrow."

"Goodnight."

He walked off and slipped out the door. She

waited a moment, and then headed toward the elevator on shaky legs. That kiss had done more to shake her up than anything he'd said.

She wasn't entirely sure she wanted him to kiss her again. The kiss had disturbed her in more than one way. Not that she'd had much experience kissing men, but his kiss had left her confused and shaking. *Was that what a good kiss was supposed to do?*

She'd have to ask Suki. She had a lot of things to ask Suki before she saw Rocco again.

When she reached the elevator, a man grabbed her elbow and spun her around to face him. Paul. He looked angry. Then his face turned bland, and he released her elbow and glanced back to the lobby.

"Bethany, we need to talk." His voice was insistent, low.

"Yes. Should we leave the hotel?"

"No. You've drawn too much attention to yourself for us to leave now."

"Then come up to my room."

"Your room." He raised an eyebrow. "Are you sure?"

"Yes. It's the only place inside this hotel where we can speak in private. Only, I don't have a key."

"Simple. Go to the front desk and request a new one."

"I didn't think of that. Be right back." She headed for the front desk.

When she'd obtained a new key and come back,

Paul wasn't by the elevator. Puzzled, she looked about, but she didn't see him anywhere. Had he gone up to her floor to wait for her?

She pressed the button. *Only one way to find out.*

When the elevator opened, it was full. People poured out, and Bethany stepped in. An older couple followed her into the car, and then Paul stepped in as well. He didn't make eye contact with her. No, he ignored her completely and watched the numbers as the elevator rose.

They rode up to the fifth floor and got off. He turned the other direction and didn't turn back until the elevator door closed. By then, she'd opened the door to her room with the new key. In only seconds, he was by her side, scanning the room. Then they were both inside.

Wearing a scowl, he closed the door and stood with his arms folded. "What the hell were you thinking?"

"Paul, what do you mean?"

"I told you to stay away from Al Capone and everyone on the fourth floor. I told you they're dangerous."

"They haven't been dangerous to me."

"All right. Start talking."

"Well, Suki gave me the prettiest gold dress and taught me how to dance. And Rocco helped me."

"I'll bet he did."

Paul's sarcasm was unmistakable. *Could he*

possibly be jealous? Had he seen Rocco kiss her? Her heart swooped high even as she backed away from him and sat on the bed.

"From the beginning. Tell me everything."

"If you want me to start at the beginning, this might take a while."

"I've got all night." He pulled up a chair across from her and lowered himself into it. "Now slow down, back up, and start at the beginning. How did you meet them?"

"Oh. Well, I met Suki while I was downstairs shopping for a new dress. I didn't have the money for one. I'd spent it all on my new haircut. So she invited me up to her room and gave me one of her dresses."

"What room were you in?"

"Four-thirty-one."

Paul closed his eyes and then opened them again. "Capone is in four-thirty-three. You were just two doors down from him."

"Well, Frank's in four-thirty-two, I think. He's Suki's boyfriend. She has her own room."

"I know who they are." His voice rose. "What part of *stay away from the fourth floor* did you not understand?"

"I just thought that since I was with Suki, everything would be all right. She's really nice."

Paul closed his eyes again as if what she'd said pained him, then opened them and gave her a look of frustration. "Suki is a gangster's moll. You're in just as much danger palling around with her, whether she's nice or not."

"Maybe you're wrong. Maybe she isn't part of all that."

"She is. Capone bought out the whole floor. Everyone on that floor is connected with him in some way."

Bethany pulled off her shoes and let them fall to the ground. The day had been long, and she was comfortable with Paul. She had been from the moment she'd met him.

His expression changed once she took off her shoes, and he seemed to struggle with something. "Go on. What happened then?"

"Well, I had a date with Mr. Rivalde Friday night. I'd promised him before I met you and really didn't want to go."

"You didn't want to go?"

"No, not after I..." She let the word trail away.

His deep brown eyes never left her face.

"Well, anyway, I'd promised. We went to see Valentino in *The Son of the Sheik.*"

He nodded. Everyone knew about that movie.

"We walked to the theater. I enjoyed the show, until he tried to--" She broke off and winced. "Well he--"

"What'd he do, Bethany?" Paul asked in a low, controlled growl.

"H-he put his hands all over me, and I didn't know how to make him stop. I got scared and ran out of the theater toward the hotel. Then I ran into Rocco." She stopped for a breath, looked into Paul's eyes, and found him staring at her with both jealousy and anger. She dropped her voice to a whisper. "He said he'd take care of me and make sure nobody else bothered me."

"He'll do that. He'll keep other men away. But then who'll protect you from Rocco?"

She opened her mouth to speak, and then closed it again.

"He's not some college boy you can say no to. He's a very dangerous man."

"He'd never hurt me. He said he wants to take care of me."

"You haven't met his other girlfriends, have you?"

She shook her head.

"It's just a matter of time until you're a gangster's moll like Suki."

"I'm nobody's moll."

"You're keeping company with Rocco, accepting his gifts. He'll expect payment soon. He expects it."

"You make it sound dreadful, like I've sold myself."

"Haven't you? What are you going to do? Turn him down? You think you'll hand him back his gifts and walk away? He's not like your Mr. Rivalde. He won't take so kindly to your saying no. He won't be a gentleman about it."

"Mr. Rivalde wasn't kind or a gentleman. He wouldn't keep his hands to himself. He was all over me in the movie theater. He had his hand up my dress, and if I hadn't run, if Rocco hadn't saved me when he did..."

Paul stood, curled his hands into fists, and paced toward the window. "The only reason Rocco saved you was so he could have you for himself."

"You sound as if you're jealous."

Paul refused to answer her, but he clenched his jaw.

She got up and hurried over to him. "Oh, Paul, please don't be angry with me. I didn't know he was going to kiss me downstairs. It took me by surprise." Tears filled her eyes. "Please don't be angry."

He turned and took her arms in a firm grip, but not hard enough to hurt, then looked down into her eyes. "I just want you to be safe."

She placed her hands against his chest, gazed up into his dark eyes, and blinked her tears away.

"Don't cry." He pulled her closer.

She gave him a smile even as a tear rolled down her cheek. He bent to kiss her and met her lips with a tender touch. Soft and gentle. She melted into his arms. Their breathing matched as he moved his lips across hers in a slow, sweet caress.

She rose up onto her toes, moved her hands to

the back of his neck, and held on tight. He wrapped his arms around her and brought her even closer.

Her breath caught, and he pulled away from her lips, their noses close, and his smile spread. Tenderness filled his eyes.

"Oh, Paul," she whispered on a breath. She'd never known a kiss could be like that. In his arms, she felt as if she'd come home. If only he could hold her like this forever.

"I'm not angry at you. I'm angry at this situation. It can't continue. You have to stay away from Rocco. Promise me." He searched her eyes.

How could she have ever even thought of being with anyone but Paul? From the moment she'd met him, she'd thought about him constantly, wondered where he was and what he was doing. Wondered if he liked her. All her doubts disappeared now that he'd kissed her and the answers to her questions filled his eyes.

She nodded. "I'll stay away from him, Paul. I promise."

"Good."

Someone knocked on the door. "Bethany Marie?"

Paul released her and she stepped away, her hand covering her mouth.

"Oh, no," she whispered. "It's my uncle."

CHAPTER TEN

"You'd best answer the door."

She gave Paul a worried glance. "Don't worry."

She walked over to the door and opened it. "Yes, Uncle James?"

"Who are you entertaining in your room so late at night?" He looked past her at Paul and his face darkened.

Paul stepped forward. He pulled out his badge and showed it to him."Paul Tollick, sir. Chicago Police Department."

Uncle James looked at the badge and grunted, but still scowled. He turned his frown to Bethany and looked her up and down, but she knew nothing appeared amiss other than she'd kicked off her shoes. A habit she also did at home in the evening.

He turned his attention back to Paul. "It's rather

inappropriate for you to be in my niece's room alone at night, don't you think? Even if you are here on official police business."

"Yes, sir. I agree." Paul inclined his head. "However, I cannot meet with your niece in the public areas of this hotel. I would draw too much attention to myself."

"You should have set up a meeting with her guardians present. Instead, you endangered her reputation by meeting her alone in her room. I should file a complaint."

"I don't need a guardian present," Bethany interrupted. "I'm of age now, remember?"

Uncle James turned to Bethany and his gaze zeroed in on her new necklace. "Where did those pearls come from? You haven't the money to purchase such things."

"They were a gift."

His frown deepened into a scowl. "A gift from whom?"

"Rocco."

"Rocco. Is he one of the men you met after you left the theater the other night?"

"That's right."

"Return the gift."

"I can't."

Paul cleared his throat. "Your niece has attracted the attention of a dangerous man, sir. If she returns the pearls, it's best if she leave town right afterward.

How many more days do you plan to stay in Hot Springs?"

"We leave a week from today."

"She can't stay that long. He won't leave her alone now that she's accepted his gift."

"He said he'd call me tomorrow," Bethany said.

Both men turned to look at her.

"You can take the call," Paul said in a stern voice. "But you're not to meet with him."

"Absolutely not." Her uncle agreed with Paul. "You've gotten yourself in enough trouble already, young lady."

"Did he say when he'd call?" Paul asked her, ignoring uncle James.

"No. I have no idea when he might do so."

"If he wants to see you, put him off." He paced, his hands behind his back. "Claim illness or previous plans with your aunt and uncle. And call me immediately afterward."

"Yes. I will."

Uncle James cleared his throat. "It's late. If you have no other questions for my niece..."

"None that can't wait until tomorrow." Paul tipped his hat to Bethany, and then acknowledged her uncle. "Mr. Robinson."

Her uncle inclined his head, and Paul let himself out.

Uncle James then turned to her and gestured with his hand.

"Sit down." He pulled the chair closer to where she sat on the bed and dropped down into it. Taking a deep breath he exhaled. "You wanted to know about your inheritance."

"Yes, I do." She leaned forward. He was finally going to tell her.

"Bethany, you know I only want what's best for you."

"Yes, sir."

"Your aunt and I have tried to guide you."

She nodded.

"I'm concerned about this situation. Only a matter of days before you come of age, and you take up with criminals. Now I find a policeman talking to you alone in your room. Do you understand my concern?"

"Yes."

"It's completely inappropriate for you to be alone in your room with any man, even a policeman. Once again you have sent a wrong message. If that man touched you... laid his hands upon you..."

Bethany thought of Paul's kiss and blushed.

"Answer me, Bethany," her uncle growled. "If he has touched you inappropriately, I'll have his badge and his head, too."

"No, no." Bethany shook her head. "Please don't cause trouble for Paul. He's a good man. He hasn't done anything wrong."

"I'll not have men pawing you. I don't care who they are."

"Paul isn't the one who pawed me. Your friend Mr. Rivalde is."

"Paul." His eyes narrowed. "So you're on a first name basis with him. That's it. I'm filing a complaint."

"But he didn't do anything wrong."

"It was a good thing I arrived when I did, before things progressed any further, as I'm sure they would have. You seem determined to ruin your good name."

"You don't care that Mr. Rivalde pawed me in the theater." Bethany stood and clenched her fists. *"He's* the one who laid his hands on *me.* Yet you won't believe me when I tell you he did, and you're not listening to me now, either. Paul didn't do anything wrong."

"I have known Mr. Rivalde for many years. And I know his character. *You* are the one who has been running about town half dressed, taking up with men we know nothing about. I warned you how men would treat you if you insist on dressing like that."

"Oh, so you're blaming me for *everything?* While your friend remains blameless. You've known me a lot longer than you've known him, I'll bet."

"Bethany, your behavior of late has been unreliable, as has your word. Telling your aunt you would rest in the room and then getting your hair cut off, saying you would be out with Mr. Rivalde, and then running off with gangsters and staying out half the night. You cannot expect me to rely on your word when you have behaved this way."

She threw her hands up in the air. "Believe what you want then. Since you don't believe me anyway."

Arguing with him was pointless, and she was tired.

"Obviously, you can no longer wander around unescorted. I think it's best if you stay with your aunt at all times from now until we leave town. Your aunt has gone to bed feeling unwell. It's likely your willful, selfish behavior this evening brought on her headache. If you hadn't gone down to the bar and instead done what your aunt had told you, you wouldn't have gotten yourself into this predicament."

Bethany stared at her feet, noting the small hole in the toe of her stocking, wishing he would just leave. She *was* in a predicament, and she had gotten herself into it, but she didn't need him to point that out and treat her like a child.

"Your aunt is scheduled for another treatment tomorrow and I expect you to accompany her. Having another treatment at the spa tomorrow won't hurt you."

"All right." *But what about my inheritance?* She wanted to blurt out the question, but knew that would be foolish now. Growing impatient, she waited.

"Now, about the money you'll inherit."

Unable to help herself, she scooted to the edge of the bed.

"You must understand that most of it is tied up in stocks and bonds and various holdings. It's not sitting stacked up in bills in some dusty vault waiting for you to use it at will. I will explain everything to you once we return home. Financial matters are complex and may not be easy for you to grasp. They require a person who understands such things, who can manage your money and make it grow instead of letting it dwindle away. Do you understand?"

"Yes, sir." She nodded; partly dismayed that she couldn't go right out and treat herself to new clothes and a fancy dinner so she could eat as much as she wanted.

"Your aunt and I believe Mr. Rivalde would be a good man to manage your holdings and make you a good husband. We'd hoped you'd accept his proposal."

"I'm sure you were disappointed, but I can't marry him."

"He won't be the only one to propose, now that you've come into money. You'll have suitors aplenty. They'll be drawn by the money. You have no idea whether or not those men were drawn by the knowledge of what you've just inherited. With Richard, though, we know that's not the case and he has his own solid portfolio. We do have plans for a merger. He's a good businessman and would take good care of you."

"So we are talking about a lot of money. Are you telling me I'm rich?"

Uncle James nodded.

"How rich?"

"Rich enough. You'll see the balance sheet soon enough. Then you'll know."

"Isn't your friend Mr. Rivalde also drawn by the money? Doesn't that make *him* just the same as any of the other suitors you claim I'm going to have?"

"I've known Richard for years. He's a trusted businessman with his own holdings. I can't say the same for the young men of today who drive about in their fancy new cars and blow piles of money on their wild lifestyles. That Rocco fellow is obviously drawn to money as all gangsters are. And as for the policeman, they don't make much money. Richard is obviously a better choice."

Her uncle's reasonable tone got on her nerves.

Bethany didn't see how any of what he'd just said made Mr. Rivalde appear to be a better man. *He wanted her money, too, for that merger.* She just knew it.

"Well, I'm not going to marry him. I don't like him enough to marry him. *Ever.*"

Her uncle stood. "I suggest you go to sleep now. It's nearly two."

"Yes. It's late, and I'm tired."

He walked to the door, and then paused before opening it. "If you'd accept Richard's marriage proposal, the problem with these gangsters and the policeman would all go away. We'd announce your engagement, and that would put an end to it. Something you should think about."

"Goodnight, Uncle James."

"Goodnight." He let himself out.

She walked over to the door, locked it, and pushed what her uncle had said out of her thoughts. Her thoughts as she changed into her nightgown and slipped into bed were of Paul and the moments they'd shared before they had been interrupted. She reached up with her fingertips and touched her lips. Paul had kissed her. She wanted to savor the memory and the feeling forever. Their first kiss. A night she'd always remember.

She smiled beneath her fingertips. She wanted to remember each second, longed to store the feelings inside her heart and relive the memory of his kiss.

She'd wished for it when she'd blown out the candles on her birthday cake. She'd wished Paul would kiss her. She'd wondered what it would feel like if he did. And when he did, it was so much better than she ever could have imagined. The very best part of her birthday.

Oh, why hadn't she met Paul before she'd agreed to a date with Mr. Rivalde? If she hadn't gone out on that date, none of this would've happened. She wouldn't have met Rocco.

Her nerves were on edge. What would she tell Rocco tomorrow when he called? He'd understand if she told him she was going down to the baths. Suki had said she took a treatment twice a week when she was in town. Besides, Bethany had told Rocco she'd come to Hot Springs with her aunt and uncle for the baths. So it wouldn't look as if she were avoiding him. That's what she'd do. It would buy her one day, at least.

She curled up on her side and tried to drift off to sleep, but hours passed before sleep came to her. She was rich and in love with Paul, a gangster thought she was his new moll, and her uncle's friend wanted to marry her.

Too many thoughts ran through her mind for her to sleep well.

Her thoughts kept returning to Paul's kiss.

The MAINTENANCE MAN arrived early to finish repairing the phone.

Minutes after he left, the phone rang. It was her aunt, speaking in a clipped voice. "Be ready for breakfast in thirty minutes."

"All right," Bethany said. Then she hung up.

She was nearly ready for breakfast when the phone rang again.

"Hello?"

"Good morning, doll."

"Rocco?"

"Who else would it be?" A challenge filled his voice.

"You sound different on the phone."

"Yeah?" He lowered his voice. "Well, you sound like a kitten who's still in bed."

"Oh, no. I'm up, getting ready to have breakfast with my aunt. Then we both have spa treatments."

"Enjoy yourself, doll. I'll pick you up later this evening and take you to dinner. It'll be late. I have a meeting."

"What time is your meeting?" The more information she could get out of Rocco, the better she could help Paul do his job.

He hesitated. "It might be over by eight. You be a good kitten and wait by the phone."

"All right." She could use the excuse of having a headache. Say the hot baths had given her a bad one, and she needed to rest.

"Just all right? No pouting, kitten. I'll make it up to you. I'll take you somewhere nice and private."

"I'm wearing the pearls you gave me." She was a terrible liar. Could he tell by her voice she didn't want to go to dinner with him? "They're so pretty."

At least that was honest. Easier to say that than to pretend she looked forward to a private dinner with him. The pearls were pretty and she did like them, even though she knew she couldn't keep them. She'd enjoy them until she had to give them back.

"Doll face, that's just the beginning. I told you I'd treat you right. Think of me when you wear them."

"Yes, Rocco." That wasn't so hard. Saying it was close enough to the *yes, sir* and *yes, ma'am* she'd said to her aunt and uncle since she was small.

"That's what I like to hear, doll. You be a good kitten. I have to go."

They each said goodbye, and then she hung up the phone and sat motionless on the bed. How many days and nights could she keep this up? She couldn't put off Rocco forever. No way would she make it until Sunday when they left. What was she going to do?

She picked up the phone and called Paul.

"Bethany." A smile filled his voice once she said his name. "How are you this morning?"

"I didn't get much sleep, so I'm tired. Rocco just called."

"What'd he say?"

She repeated the conversation for him word for word. He listened in silence. When she was done, he said, "You can't have dinner with him tonight."

"I don't want to have dinner with him."

"Good. Find an excuse not to."

"I can beg off with a headache, but that'll only get me through today. I don't know what I'll do tomorrow."

"I'll think of something. Be patient."

"Okay, I'll try."

"What time is your appointment today?"

"I don't have one. I'm going with my aunt at one o'clock, hoping they can fit me in."

"Good. I'll find you later."

THE DAY WENT SMOOTHLY ENOUGH. Her aunt ordered them grapefruit and toast for breakfast, but for once Bethany didn't mind. She'd lost her appetite thinking of Rocco and what he might do if she tried to pull away from him. Her stomach turned end over end.

The bath treatment helped take her mind away from everything for a while. Then while she waited for her aunt to finish her treatments at the Fordyce, Paul found her.

The clock was about to strike four, the time of day that sometimes made her sleepy, and she sat in the music room enjoying the sunlight filtering through the stained glass when suddenly he stood in front of her.

His deep brown eyes drank her in, the hidden emotion in them for only her to see.

"How was your treatment?" he asked.

She smiled. "Good, thank you."

"Walk with me."

She stood and walked beside him as he made casual conversation. "Do you feel any older now that you've had your birthday?"

"Positively ancient." She laughed, and he paused to look at her.

"Positively beautiful. Far from ancient." He gave her a smile. "Come for a walk with me outside."

"That sounds lovely."

They left the music room and headed downstairs, but instead of going outside he took her down to the basement, a cool, quiet space.

One he assured himself they were alone, his expression turned serious. "We have a new development."

"A development?" Confused, she wrinkled her nose and forehead.

"Police just pulled a man's body out of Lake Catherine. He'd been shot four times."

"Oh, that's awful."

"The man is Suki's boyfriend, Frank."

Bethany gasped and stared at Paul wide-eyed. "No."

CHAPTER ELEVEN

"Yes. No question that it's Frank. You won't hear about it in the papers or on the radio. They'll keep it quiet as long as they can, but it's true."

"Poor Suki."

"Suki can take care of herself. I'm more worried about you."

"Me?"

"Listen, and I'll explain the way these things play out. Someone killed a member of Capone's gang, and they'll retaliate. I don't want you anywhere near any of those men -- and that includes your boyfriend, Rocco."

"He's *not* my boyfriend. You know he's not."

"He doesn't see it that way. When he called you, did he give any indication he knew about Frank's death?"

"No, not at all."

"That should show you Rocco's two faces, if nothing else does, because Capone's gang is well aware of what happened to Frank. He knew about it when he called you."

"Oh." She widened her eyes and shook her head. "He's quite an actor then, isn't he?"

"They all are, sweetheart. Don't let it make you feel foolish. They would've taken in anyone with your trusting nature."

He had no idea how much better that made her feel. Or perhaps he did. She'd been kicking herself and feeling like a little fool ever since she'd accepted the pearls from Rocco. She'd let him turn her head by giving her something glamorous.

"We can't stay down here much longer. Your aunt will finish her treatment and wonder where you are."

"I know."

He cupped her chin and bent to kiss her. His lips were as tender as they'd been the night before and she leaned in, wanting more, wanting to be closer.

He wrapped his arms around her and pulled her against him. She felt safe, warm, and loved within his embrace. She parted her lips, and he slipped his tongue between them, a slow, gentle, teasing movement, and she wanted more. She touched her tongue to his and they began a slow dance, a long, lingering kiss that left them both breathless.

When they finally pulled apart, they searched each other's eyes. Neither of them needed to say a word. They both smiled at each other at the same time.

Being with him felt so right.

"We'd better go." He broke the shared silence.

"Yes," she said, but she didn't want to go. "I wish we didn't have to."

"Me, too." A noise overhead had him looking over his shoulder. "I'll see you to the top of the stairs, then you should go meet your aunt."

Bethany reached her hand out to his, and he enfolded it within his larger, stronger one.

They climbed the stairs together.

ALL THE WAY back to the hotel, Bethany thought about Suki.

Bethany had to see her. Suki had been good to Bethany, and now she'd lost the man she loved. Though Paul wanted her to stay away from everyone on the fourth floor, Suki was her friend. She should be there when Suki needed her. Besides, now that Suki's boyfriend was dead, she no longer had a connection to Al Capone. Frank had been her connection.

Once Bethany and her aunt reached their destination, Bethany told Aunt Margaret that she had to return a book she'd borrowed from the library. Then she headed back out again after promising her aunt she'd come right back to the hotel.

She dropped off the book, and then hurried back to the hotel and up to the fourth floor. This time, two men in dark suits and hats stood in the hallway as she walked up to Suki's door. Bethany knocked twice before Suki opened the door.

"Bethany." Suki stood just inside, darting her gaze frantically up and down the hall. "Come in. Hurry."

Bethany slipped through the door, and Suki closed and locked it.

"Is it true? Is Frank really dead?" Bethany asked, although from Suki's appearance, she knew it had to be true.

"Yes." Suki's eyes were red from crying, and dark mascara stains marred the area beneath her eyes. "They shot him in the back. Rocco said he never saw it coming."

"How?"

"It's better if you don't know any more than that. He was doing something the boss sent him to do. That's all I know. Even that was too much. The police questioned me, and so did Mr. Capone." She glanced at Bethany, her eyes bright. "It's best to just be a pretty girl, the life of the party, arm candy that lights up a room, but not so bright that you notice things. See?"

Bethany nodded.

"You remember that."

She gave a slight frown. She didn't ever want to be in the position Suki was in now.

"We had plans, Frank and me." Suki's voice hitched. "He promised to take me to the opera. I've always wanted to see one, and he said he'd pick up the tickets once the job was done. Only, he never came back."

"Oh, Suki. I'm so sorry."

"Yeah." Suki paced to the window and reached for her flask. "I'm sorry, too."

She gulped from the flask, and Bethany wondered if it contained the same kind of rum Suki always drank. If so, she wondered how Suki could gulp it down like that.

"Opera is probably overrated anyway." She turned to Bethany. "You want some?"

"No, thanks."

"I don't know what I'm gonna do now. I've got to find myself a new sugar daddy, and soon."

"I thought you loved Frank."

"I did, but Frank's dead. What am I going to do now? A girl's gotta eat."

"Don't you have any money?"

"Not enough to last. Frank took real good care of me, but I didn't want him to leave me holding the bag. So I didn't get involved in his business." She shrugged and wiped the mascara from beneath her eyes with a hanky embroidered with the letter *F*. She glanced at it, blinked twice, and threw it onto the dresser. "Come on. We'll go dancing at the club."

"I don't know, Suki. Wouldn't it be better for you to stay out of sight? If the police or whoever killed Frank is watching you..."

"Let 'em watch. I just want to put on my glad rags, dance, and have a ball," Suki said. "Life's too damn short."

"Wish I could go dancing with you, but I've already promised Rocco I'd wait for him to call. He's taking me to dinner tonight."

"Oh, in that case, you'd better wait by the phone. Never be someplace other than where Rocco tells you to be."

Bethany frowned. "Why?"

"You're so wet behind the ears." Suki sighed. "You just do whatever Rocco tells you to do, and you'll be fine. He'll take good care of you. But never make him angry. Understand?"

Bethany nodded. "Yes."

"Good girl." Suki swept a red dress off the back of a chair and handed it to Bethany. "Here. Wear this tonight. Red is his favorite color, and you'll want to take his mind off things to keep him in a good mood. Whatever you do, keep him in a good mood."

"Thank you."

"Go on now. You'd better be in your room in case he calls to check on you."

"Are you going to be all right?"

"You're sweet, but you don't need to worry about me, doll. I'm like a cat. Always land on my feet. Go on now."

Bethany nodded and slipped out the door, closing it softly behind her. The men in the hallway studied her as she walked to the elevator, and she tried to act as if the only thing she'd come for was to visit and borrow a dress. She released a breath after the elevator closed.

Never again would she have to return to the fourth floor.

THE PHONE RANG, and Bethany picked it up. "Hello?"

"Pack your bags, doll. We're leaving town."

"What?" Shocked, Bethany held on to the phone. She had expected Rocco to tell her about their dinner plans so she could beg off with a headache. Instead, he was leaving, and he expected her to go with him. A chill ran up her spine. "When?"

"In about an hour."

"Where are we going?"

"Just have your bags packed and ready."

Click. He'd hung up. He hadn't even asked if she wanted to go. Hadn't waited for her to tell him yes or no. *His voice had contained none of the patience or toler-ance he'd displayed before.* He'd given her a command

and expected her to do exactly as he said. After what Suki had told her, that frightened her. She didn't want to make Rocco angry. So what should she do?

She paced across the room. Her leaving with him wasn't something she and Rocco had talked about. In fact, they hadn't talked much at all. Bethany stopped and looked out the window. *Where was he going?* He hadn't told her where.

She couldn't go with him. He'd ordered her around as if he owned her, but she'd never agreed to this.

She didn't want to be anywhere around Rocco when he found out she wasn't going. *He'd be angry.* She barely knew him, but she knew that much about him, and she hadn't liked the glimpse she'd gotten into Suki's way of life. *At first, it had appeared to be fun and glamorous, but Paul was right. It was dangerous, and these men were very dangerous.*

If only she hadn't run into Rocco the day she'd run from the theater. If only she'd run into Paul instead.

Reaching for the phone, she dialed his room and prayed he'd answer. *He'd know what to do. He always knew what to do.*

Unfortunately, the phone rang and rang and no one picked up.

Her aunt and uncle had just left to have dinner in the dining room. Bethany couldn't call Suki. So she continued to pace, and then called Paul again with no luck.

Before an hour passed, Rocco knocked on her door. She opened it wearing her nightgown and robe, planning to tell him she didn't feel well.

He stepped inside, closed the door, took one look at her, and said, "What the hell is this?"

"I-I'm not feeling so well. It must've been the heat of the bath. My head's pounding."

He furrowed his brow into a deep frown and glanced about the room, then loomed over her. "You haven't packed."

"No, I've been lying down, trying to get rid of my headache."

He scowled at her. "You were fine when you went to see Suki."

"It came on after I was back in the room."

"I don't have time for this." He walked over to the corner, picked up her suitcase, and tossed it onto the bed. "Pack. Now."

Widening her eyes, she backed away from him.

"Do I need to repeat myself?"

"No, no," she whispered. "I'll pack."

She started putting her things into the suitcase and reached for the red dress.

He saw the dress and grunted, as if he knew where it had come from. Well, of course he did. He knew she'd been to see Suki. Those men guarding the hallway were observant, and the red dress was hard to miss.

Trying to soften his mood she said, "I'd planned to wear this dress to dinner tonight. Suki said red is your favorite color."

"You can change into that after we get there. Put that one on." He pointed to her gold dress. "But hurry up. I ain't got all day."

She took the dress into the bathroom and closed the door. Looking into the mirror, she saw how pale her face was. If only she'd been able to reach Paul. She pulled the dress over her head just before Rocco swung the door open and looked her up and down.

She reached for the stockings hanging by the sink to dry and walked past him to the suitcase, pretending to be interested in packing when all she wanted was to run away from him and this room and wherever he planned to take her.

"I'll need to leave a note for my aunt and uncle."

"No note."

She gulped and turned to face him.

"You can call them in a day or two."

"Thank you," she whispered. Then she went into the bathroom for her toiletries. When she was done, she closed the suitcase and looked at him.

"Your shoes." He gestured toward them, and she walked over and slid them on.

Then he picked up the suitcase, put his arm around her waist, and headed for the door. Her heart raced when he first touched her and then swept her along beside him.

How would she get away? How could she get word to Paul and her aunt and uncle? *Where was he taking her?* What would happen to her when they got there?

Downstairs, they swept out of the elevator and out the doors toward a shiny black car waiting at the curb. Two other cars sat behind it.

As Bethany slid across the seat, she couldn't help but notice how different sliding into the back seat felt now. Rocco displayed none of the gentlemanly behavior he'd shown her before when he'd held her hand, acted as her protector, and rescued her from Mr. Rivalde.

Rocco went around to the other side, opened the door, and got in. He shoved a violin case over next to Bethany so that it sat on the floor between them.

Why wasn't the violin case in the trunk with the other suitcases? She looked at Rocco's hands and fingers. He didn't appear to have the hands of a violinist.

He flipped the latch on the case, opened it, and pulled out a large black gun.

Bethany's whole body stiffened, and she clutched the edge of the seat.

He glanced at her. "You thought I had a violin, didn't you?"

Too frightened to speak, she nodded.

"The rule in Hot Springs is that we have to lay down our guns. We always keep them handy, though." He grinned and opened his jacket pocket to reveal a holstered pistol.

She widened her eyes.

"It's a Colt nineteen-seventeen. It makes a lot of sweet music, but the big one stops 'em dancing cold."

Speechless, she stared at him.

"You scared? You look like you've never seen a gun."

She shook her head.

"This one's a Thompson Submachine Gun." He laid it across his lap and casually touched the barrel. "You can touch it if you want. Here, put your hand on it."

He reached for her hand and pulled it over to lay it on the gun. The cold hard metal beneath her fingertips made her want to jerk her hand away, but he kept his hand firm on hers. He moved her hand up and down. "Stroke it, like that. That's it, baby. Up and down."

"What the hell are you doing back there, Rocco?" the driver growled from the front seat. "Pay attention. This ain't no petting party."

"Just showing her the gun." Rocco released Bethany's hand, and she pulled it back into her lap and pressed her other hand over it to stop it from shaking. "You remember your first time, Joey. Nothing like that cold, hard steel."

"Yeah, well... you got plenty of time to show her whatever you got to show her on the drive. For now, keep your eyes sharp."

Rocco said, "Sit back and relax, doll. We got a long drive ahead of us. Like I said, I'll take good care of you. Just wanted you to know that I got the muscle to do it."

He was a dangerous man, and he'd brought her right into the middle of whatever was going on. She looked around at the other cars and noted that the other men had also taken out guns. Guns they'd kept hidden. Their expressions and movements had changed as well, sending a clear signal that they were armed and dangerous. *Clearly they were no longer on vacation.*

Paul's words about Rocco came back to Bethany. *He'll keep other men away, but who'll protect you from Rocco?*

He'd seemed like a gentleman at first, with his good manners, his fancy suits, and his expensive lifestyle, but now she'd gotten a glimpse of the real Rocco, and what she'd seen had frightened her.

As the car rolled out of town, fear rolled through her veins. She'd never been more terrified in her life.

ethany hadn't seen Suki. *They hadn't taken her with them.* No, Bethany was all alone, surrounded by gangsters with guns, and she had no idea where Rocco might take her or what he'd do to her once they got there.

Her heart cried out for Paul as she closed her eyes and leaned back against the seat, hiding beneath the pretense of having a headache and trying to shut it all out. Even as she tried to pretend she was calm, however, her heart raced, her mouth went dry, and terror gripped her.

They were nearly out of town when a police car pulled them over. She opened her eyes and peered out the window.

"What do they want?" the driver asked the other man in the front seat. Rocco hadn't bothered to introduce her to any of the other men keeping company with Mr. Capone.

He shifted his gun from the casual position on his lap to an active one, sticking the barrel out the window and resting his hand near the trigger.

"It ain't like them to stop us for anything. It's a message for Mr. Capone."

The men kept their guns visible as the policeman walked toward Mr. Capone's car.

It was Paul.

He'd come for her, wearing a uniform belonging to the local police. Bethany's heart beat faster. She forced away her surprise and closed her eyes. *No, no, no. They'll shoot him. He came to rescue me, but they'll shoot him.*

If that happened, her heart would never recover. She opened her eyes and focused on his face. This might be the last time she ever saw him, so she wanted to memorize his face, every feature.

He approached their car and said to the driver, "Do you have a Miss Robinson in here?"

"Yeah." Rocco narrowed his eyes and fingered his gun as if he'd like to use it. "But she's with me, and she's of age now."

"That's not why I need to bring her in." Paul turned his gaze on Bethany. "Miss, if you'll step out of the car, these men can be on their way. We don't want to slow Mr. Capone down any more than we have to."

Bethany reached for the door handle.

"Wait a minute," Rocco said. "What do you want with her?"

"The sheriff has some questions for her. Nothing to do with any of you."

Mr. Capone's driver honked his horn. A signal that Mr. Capone had grown impatient.

Rocco deepened his scowl and looked at Bethany. "Go on. I can't come with you. I'll call you later, doll."

"All right." She opened the door and stepped out on shaky legs.

Paul walked over to her, took her arm in a firm grip, and led her over to the patrol car. Before they reached it, the drivers of the other cars hit the gas and raced off down the road. Within moments, the line of black cars was out of sight.

He opened the door for her and she got in, her whole body shaking.

"Oh, Paul. I was so scared."

"I know, baby." He put his arm around her and pulled her close, then kissed her once on the forehead. "I don't know what I would've done if anything had happened to you."

"How did you know?"

"I've been watching them. I thought you were safe until Rocco hustled you into the car."

"I tried to call you."

"I was working, baby. Thought you'd stay in your room until tomorrow."

"How'd you get this car and the uniform?"

"I'm a man of many talents." He winked at her and unbuttoned his shirt. "Time to change back, though. We'll have to leave the car here."

"How will we get back?"

"I thought we'd walk, if you don't mind. That'll give us plenty of time to talk."

"Yes, I'd like that. My aunt and uncle must be worried."

"Then perhaps your uncle will see the sense of your leaving town earlier than he'd planned. Especially since Rocco might come back to look for you."

"Oh, but I don't want to go." She placed her hand on his arm. "I want to stay here with you."

"My work here is done." He covered her hand with one of his and gave it a slight squeeze before letting go. "I'll have to leave soon, too."

"Oh, I see." Her hand dropped away. "Now that they're gone..."

"Yes." He nodded.

Sadness filled her at the thought of being apart from him. He removed the uniform shirt and reached for his own shirt. She took in the muscles of his shoulders and arms as he stood wearing only a sleeveless white undershirt. The urge to run her hands up his arms and shoulders came over her, but her shyness won out and she held back.

Blushing, she glanced at the ground, traced a half circle with the toe of her shoe, and waited for him to put his shirt on.

"I want you safely away from here and out of Rocco's reach as soon as possible."

"I understand," she said softly, her head still down.

Dressed now, he said in a quiet voice, "Penny for your thoughts."

"I wish we had more time together." She gazed back up into his eyes.

He reached for her hand, threaded his fingers through hers, and said, "Let's make the most of the time we have and enjoy this walk."

"Yes." She smiled.

He tightened his fingers around hers as they walked toward town. Her heart soared at the simple act of holding hands. She wanted to memorize the way his eyes softened whenever he looked into her eyes. Wanted to remember every detail of his face and the sound of his voice, so she could carry it with her forever.

If this was goodbye, she wanted it to stretch out as long as she could. She didn't want to think of the word, didn't want to say it.

After they had walked along for a few moments, she stopped.

"Wait. There's something I have to do." She pulled her hand free, reached for the pearl necklace, and pulled it over her head.

"I never want to see this again," she said. "I'll leave it at the front desk with a note for Rocco, and they can deliver it to him when he returns. I can't stand to have it touching my skin."

"I'll keep it until we get there, so you won't have to touch it." Paul held out his hand.

She handed him the necklace. He placed it in his pocket, and when he brought his hand back out, he held another box wrapped in pink paper.

"I bought this for you for your birthday, but wasn't sure if you'd want it."

"A gift from you, Paul?" Bethany clasped her hands together. "Of course I want it."

She held out her hands, and he handed her the present. She tore off the paper as fast as she could and opened the box.

Inside was a pair of silver and blue earrings in the shape of two delicate butterflies.

"Oh, Paul." Bethany caught her breath. "They're beautiful."

"I'm glad you like them."

"They're Pipevine Swallowtail butterflies." She looked up at him and let a deep smile spread across her face. "From the day we met at the park."

"I wasn't sure you'd remember."

"Oh, yes. I remember. I will always remember."

"They aren't as fancy or as expensive as your other gifts."

"This is the best gift I've ever received." She put her arms around his neck. "I'll treasure them always."

He bent for a kiss, and she raised her head to meet his lips. The kiss was sweeter for the danger she'd faced down and the relief they both felt at being together. The kiss went on longer than any of the others they'd shared, and she knew she'd always remember this moment.

Each time Paul kissed her, he left her with a memory she'd treasure, hopefully all the days of her life.

"I can't wait to wear them." Bethany reached up to remove her gold earrings and replaced them with the butterfly earrings. She dropped the gold earrings into her coin purse. Looking up at Paul, she smiled. "How do I look?"

"Beautiful." He cupped her chin and took her in with a loving gaze. "They suit you."

"Oh, I can't wait until I can see them in a mirror when we get back to my hotel room."

"I'm glad you like them." He smiled. "They match your eyes."

"I wonder if the butterflies are in our special spot today."

"We can find out." He reached for her hand and together they walked toward the hotel.

As they strolled along they spoke of his life in Chicago and hers in Ohio. Of how how his father had been a dependable policeman and hers a wealthy man who enjoyed drinking and driving new cars much too fast. Both men had died too young.

They passed a store window and Bethany paused. "Oh there must be a mirror inside."

"Let's go in so you can see them on."

Bethany beamed up at him as the earrings dangled by her ears. Paul pushed open the door, which jangled the bell above it, and they entered.

A sales clerk approached. "Can I help you?"

"We'd like to borrow your mirror for a minute."

"Yes, of course." She gestured to a mirror on the side wall. "Over there. And if there's anything I can help you with please let me know."

Bethany walked over and viewed herself in the mirror. The delicate butterfly earrings were perfect and the blue did match her eyes.

"Oh, Paul, they're perfect. Just perfect." Eyes sparkling she turned back toward him. "I love them."

He took her hand in his and pulled her closer. "And I love you."

Her heart fluttered. "Oh Paul, I love you too."

He bent down brushing her lips with a soft kiss and then said; "Now let's go to our special place and see about those butterflies."

"Yes, I'd like that."

Holding hands they left the store and headed for the hill with the balustrade bandstand hill where they'd first met.

When they reached the spot, he stopped.

"This is where it all began." He touched one of her butterfly earrings and gently caressed her ear. "In the middle of all those butterflies is where I first saw you."

"Yes," she smiled and then sat on the same bench she'd sat on that day, arranging herself just as she'd been when he'd first seen her. She smiled up at him. "I was sitting right here, reading."

"If I could have a picture painted of anything, this is what I would want painted." He smiled. "Bethany beneath the butterflies."

They smiled at each other in silence, sharing the moment.

"Be very still," he said.

She froze, breathing softly as butterflies flitted around them, surrounding them both, reminding them of the day they had first met.

He picked a flower and tucked it into the collar of her dress. "Now, don't move. Let's wait and see what happens."

The butterflies danced in the air while Bethany basked beneath the love shining from Paul's eyes.

"You're not watching the butterflies," she said.

He smiled. "No. I'd much rather watch you."

She blushed, and a butterfly paused near the flower on her dress.

Bethany held her breath and watched the butterfly without moving her head or speaking, afraid she might scare it away. If only she could capture this moment and store it away.

Finally she whispered, "I wish we could stay here forever."

When he didn't answer, she looked up at him and searched his eyes to find a look she couldn't decipher.

Then as if he'd just realized he hadn't answered her, he sent her a loving look and said, "I was memorizing the moment. So I'll always remember."

"Oh," She breathed in and let another smile spread across her face. "Me, too."

"It seems neither of us wants this to end."

"I want to be with you, wherever you are." She couldn't keep the longing of her heart to herself. She wanted him to know how she felt.

He met her eyes. "Are you sure?"

"I'm more than sure."

"I think that can be arranged." A slow smile spread across his face. "We can discuss that in a moment. First, however..." He dropped onto one knee and leaned in to kiss her.

She melted into his kiss until she wasn't sure where she ended, and he began. Their kiss was sweet and strong, promising much for the future and expressing their gratitude at finding each other. When they broke apart, tears filled Bethany's eyes.

"Tears?" Paul cupped her chin. "We can't have that."

"They're happy tears." She laughed.

"Well in that case," he reached for her hand and helped her rise. "We can allow those."

She looked up into his eyes.

He tucked her hand in the crook of his arm and said, "Now, before we get back to the hotel, let's discuss what you want to do with the rest of your life. Now that you're of age and can choose for your-self, I want to hear what you would like to do."

They took a long walk through town and talked for hours about both her dreams and his, about ways they could be together while they pursued their dreams and of the steps they'd have to take to make it happen.

Bethany decided she wanted to go to college and become a librarian, since she always kept her nose in a book. She'd experienced enough excitement and adventure in her life already without ever having visited a foreign land. All she wanted or needed now was to have Paul by her side. He'd keep her safe, encourage her dreams, and nurture her inde-pendence.

Paul promised to leave Chicago and transfer to a police department in the town where she went to college so they could be together. She'd be far from Rocco's reach, and from the gangster's reputation of going through women, she figured he'd forget about her in time. In the meantime, Paul would be there to make sure she stayed safe.

They both wanted children, and if her aunt and uncle refused to agree to their marriage... well, Bethany didn't really need anyone's approval.

The approval shining in Paul's eyes was enough.

The End

Thank you for taking the time to read Trapping the Butterfly. If you enjoyed the story, please consider telling your friends and/or posting a review. Word of mouth is an author's best friend and much appreciated.

If you've enjoyed book one, book two is Suki's story.

Thank you for reading and reviewing! - Debra Parmley

ACKNOWLEDGMENTS

My thanks and appreciation to the staff of the Arlington Hotel; to Nalissala Allan, Park Guide at Hot Springs National Park; to Jared Kizzee and Gabe Caver of Range USA and to Charles Welshans for being my gun gurus.

Thank you to Melanie Noto, my Editor and my Cover Artist, Sheri McGathy.

Thank you also to my husband, Mike, for cooking dinner, shopping for groceries, and having the patience to put up with a wife on a book deadline, who forgets to shop or eat and even lets us run out of toilet paper.

Thank you to my readers for venturing into this 1920's world of flappers and gangsters, where anything might happen. I hope you enjoy this step into the past.

Fascinated by fairy tales and folktales, ever since she was young, Debra Parmley has always ended her stories with a happy ever after. Every story she writes turns into a romance. She started out writing gritty western historical romance and damsel in distress stories. Her first book, A Desperate Journey, was traditionally published in 2008, after competing in the American Title II contest. A hybrid author, she went on to write for five publishers before branching out with her own Indie press, Belo Dia Publishing Inc. Belo Dia is Portuguese for Beautiful Day.

Debra writes historical romance, contemporary romance, dystopian romance and romantic suspense. An Air Force veteran's wife, she writes military heroes in the present and in the future. Debra's work in the travel industry gave her the opportunity to visit many countries. Her luggage often carried home folk tales from the countries visited. Her travel experiences are scattered throughout her books. Her three favorite things are dark chocolate, visiting the beach and ocean, and hearing from her readers. Each card, letter and email is a treasured gift, like finding a perfect shell upon the beach. For more information about Debra and her books, please visit Debra's website:

http://www.debraparmley.com

Follow Debra on Book Bub:

https://www.bookbub.com/profile/debra-parmley

Newsletter sign up: http://eepurl.com/ZUyC1

Goodreads: https://www.goodreads.com/DebraParmley

FB fan page: https://www.facebook.com/authordebraparmley/

FB fan group: https://www.facebook.com/groups/debraparmley/

FB personal page: https://www.facebook.com/debra.parmley.7

Twitter: https://twitter.com/DebraParmley

Pinterest: https://www.pinterest.com/debraparmley/

Instagram: https://www.instagram.com/debraparmley/

Defensive Instructor

Marine Protector

Marine Protectors Box Set: Montana Marine; Defensive Instructor; and Marine Protector

Blind Trust

Susan Stokers Special Forces Operation Alpha series:

Protecting Pippa

Split Screen Scream

Protecting Zarifah

Contemporary Romance/military heroes:

Check Out

Aboard the Wishing Star

To Catch An Elf

Wounded Heroes Anthology

Holiday Romance:

Jenna's Christmas Wish

Dystopian Romance:

The Hunger Roads Trilogy:

A Change of Scenery: Book One

Down a Back Road: Book Two

Into the Convergence Zone: Book Three

Paranormal Romance:

Vague Directions

Poetry:

Twilight Dips